ONCE BURNED . . .

"That money was in a Swiss account," Ebony said.

"And it still is, just not in *your* Swiss account. Do you think that I couldn't find and access your money? Come on. I've found deeper hidden assets than yours. You're not nearly as clever as you think you are. So go ahead and kill me. But if you do, you will kill everything you ever worked for." Carmelita flashed Ebony a self-satisfied smile.

"It would be worth it just to see you die. But you're not getting off that easily. You see, you're going to give me all the info that I need. And I can guarantee that getting you to talk won't be a problem for me. You killed my mother, you killed my man, and you framed me. So I'm gonna make you suffer before I smoke your ass!"

Ebony took the lit end of her cigarette and placed it a millimeter away from Carmelita's cheek.

"Such a pretty face. It's a shame what I'm going to have to do to it."

Praise for the razor-sharp urban fiction of Méta Smith

"As entertaining as daytime talk show brawls. . . . The cornucopia of sex, name dropping, and hip-hop melodrama is bound to be gobbled up by fans."
—*Publishers Weekly* on *Queen of Miami*

Sex Appeal is also available as an eBook

Also by Méta Smith

Whip Appeal
Heaven's Fury
(with 50 Cent)

SEX
APPEAL

MÉTA SMITH

POCKET BOOKS

New York   London   Toronto   Sydney

Pocket Books
A Division of Simon & Schuster, Inc.
1230 Avenue of the Americas
New York, NY 10020

First Pocket Books trade paperback edition November 2009

POCKET and colophon are registered trademarks of Simon & Schuster, Inc.

For information about special discounts for bulk purchases, please contact Simon & Schuster Special Sales at 1-866-506-1949 or business@simonandschuster.com.

The Simon & Schuster Speakers Bureau can bring authors to your live event. For more information or to book an event contact the Simon & Schuster Speakers Bureau at 1-866-248-3049 or visit our website at www.simonspeakers.com.

Designed by Renata Di Biase

Manufactured in the United States of America

10 9 8 7 6 5 4 3 2 1

Library of Congress Cataloging-in-Publication Data

Smith, Méta.
  Sex appeal / by Méta Smith.
     p.   cm.
1. African American women—Fiction. 2. Rich people—Fiction. 3. Miami (Fla.)—Fiction. I. Title
  PS3619.M5922S49   2009
  813'.6—dc22   2009029418

ISBN 978-1-4165-5140-9
ISBN 978-1-4165-7997-7 (ebook)

For my "Street Team"
Taylor James
Troy James
and Jordan Smith-Berry

And for all my loyal readers . . .
Thank you for sticking with me through six books.
The best is yet to come.

ACKNOWLEDGMENTS

Thank you God, from whom all blessings flow.

Thank you to my alter ego and dissociated personality The Supreme Mistress Ebony Knight for being a part of my darkness, for flowing through me, and for showing me the light. . . .

Thank you to all the Dommes, subs, and alternative lifestyle players who helped me to write *Whip Appeal* and *Sex Appeal*. I wouldn't have had these books had it not been for your willingness to be open, your courage to go against the grain, your fetishes, your kink, your perversion, your strength, and even your weakness. It's been an amazing experience!

To my special "pets": Submit. Obey. Pay. It's the only way. Your Twisted Princess is laughing all the way to the bank. Keep it up beyotches!

To my readers for your constant support and loyalty: THANK YOU and I LOVE YOU.

Thank you to all the librarians and bookstore owners for stocking my work!

Thanks to Marc Gerald, my agent, for working so hard for me.

ACKNOWLEDGMENTS

Thanks to Megan McKeever and everyone at Simon & Schuster for your hard work and understanding.

Last but absolutely not least, I would like to thank my family and true friends for riding with me, and for loving and supporting me. *Besitos, abrazos y todo mi amor!*

Peace & Positive Vibes,
Méta

P.S. Make sure to check me out at www.MetaSmith.com!
Follow me on Twitter at Twitter.com/MetaSmith
And check me on MySpace at MySpace.com/MetaSmith

SEX
APPEAL

PROLOGUE

Money is all *that matters in this life. When you have it, the world is your oyster, and when you don't, you're a sitting duck and you have to endure whatever shots life takes at you. Don't agree? Then explain why celebrities and politicians can drive drunk, get caught with drugs, solicit hookers, have babies with mistresses, and commit all kinds of other crimes and all they receive is a slap on the wrist, while Joe Average gets put underneath the jail for lesser offenses. It's because money buys security of all kinds. Money buys favors, status, and freedom. So I did whatever it took, and I do mean whatever it took, to get rich.*

I learned the game of life from a wise and experienced master, and I played it to win. My mama was a con artist and a drug dealer who raised me in the streets, but she always wanted a better life for me. Still, Mama was a realist, she knew what I was going to be up against in life. A black woman without money may as well put a KICK ME *sign on her back and let the world line up to take shots at her ass. So Mama taught me everything that she knew about getting paid, from short cons such as panhandling and begging* softhearted people for spare change, to elaborate pyramid and Ponzi schemes. And I was good . . . very good.

But Mama, like all hustlers no matter how slick, eventually got popped. We escaped jail time by the skin of our teeth and traded the concrete jungle of Newark for the sandy shores of Miami. Mama turned her life around and I tried to, but when it boiled down to it, I reverted back to my default behavior. You know the old saying, train the child up in the way he should go and he will never stray from it? Well, it is true for the good things in life as well as the bad. I was greedy and I didn't have much of a conscience. That can be a real fucked-up combination.

Things started innocently enough. I was a struggling college student in need of cash, and my best friend hooked me up with a gig that seemed to be the answer to all my prayers. Before I knew it, I was lying, conning, and manipulating people all over again. I finessed my way from the gutter to a million-dollar empire, stepping on the hearts, spirits, and psyches of gullible and submissive men to make it to the top. It was always business, never personal. Those men got just what they asked for; they received exactly what was coming to them.

As a dominatrix to the affluent, I was paid a pretty penny by men to humiliate and degrade them, and it was all going along as right as rain, or so I thought until my best client, Erik Johansen, lost touch with reality. He became obsessed with me, threatened my life and my safety, and the life and safety of my fiancé, Jeff Cardoza. Oh, I thought I had it all together; I thought that I could handle a stupid slave and still come out on top. But I was wrong. Dead wrong.

It was like a runaway train: I saw disaster headed right for me, but I couldn't stop it. Literally, overnight my life was in shambles. Erik and Jeff were dead, and I was the main person of interest in their murders. I was the only person found alive at the gruesome scene of the crime, and my prints were the only ones found on the murder weapon. I was bloodied and disoriented; I was in such shock that I was transported to a mental hospital. If the cops had had their way, my next stop would have been jail and then death row.

I was the beneficiary of a $3 million life insurance policy that belonged to Erik Johansen, and the police saw that as enough motive for me to kill him. They believed I killed my fiancé, Jeff, because he could have ratted me out. I knew that I hadn't done either, but my mind was like a blank slate that had been wiped clean when it came to what went down the night of the murders. For days I couldn't remember anything, but I was absolutely certain of one thing: my innocence. Jeff was my soul mate, the man I was going to spend forever with. I would never have hurt him. And Erik, although he was deeply deranged and disturbed, had made me rich beyond my wildest dreams. It's true that I wanted him out of my life, but I never intended for him to lose his.

But someone on the sidelines had always wanted things to turn out as they did. A devil had definitely been at work, a demented Svengali behind the scenes who helped to create the monster that everyone thought I was. She created this mess and she committed the murders: my scheming so-called best friend, Carmelita Sanchez. In hindsight, I realized that my entire career as a dominatrix had carefully been orchestrated by her.

She pulled my strings just like a puppet master, luring me into a sadomasochistic world of bondage and domination, especially financial domination. Not only did I abuse men's bodies, I raped their wallets, and business was booming. I had Carmelita to thank for it all.

Carmelita had introduced me to Goddess Amber, the mistress who taught me everything I knew about the game and referred Erik Johansen to me. Then Erik freaked out on me and I happened to catch it all on video. I knew that Erik was in emotional turmoil, and his continuing to see me would just make things worse. The best thing I thought I could do for Erik was to cut him loose. I told him it was over, that he was no longer desired as a slave, but he refused to let me go. So, I finally agreed to go along with Carmelita's plan to blackmail him with the tape. I figured making Erik lose $10 million would turn him off for good. I was wrong. We got the money but Erik was more devoted to me than ever.

The whole thing ended with everyone I loved dead, with me in a psychiatric hospital, and with Carmelita in control of a fortune worth over $14 million. Well, I'm going to get my money, and after that I'm going to make sure that Carmelita Sanchez dies a long and painful death.

CHAPTER ONE

Florida Everglades

The smell of burning flesh mingled with a thick cloud of black smoke and filled the hallways of Everglades Psychiatric Hospital. Patients tripped and fell over one another as they attempted to escape the inferno raging throughout the facility. The sound of explosions and glass breaking mixed with people's screams and calls for help. Help didn't come fast enough.

Some of the residents choked and gasped for air as they found their way to the emergency exits. Others remained trapped in the building trying to make their way out. No practiced evacuation plan had been in place, but most of the patients were too mentally disturbed to actually follow one. By the time the fire alarm sounded, an entire wing was engulfed in flames.

There was a low rumble, like a roll of thunder, then a loud boom. Flames shot skyward and debris rained down among the evacuees outside as a group of people trapped on a balcony jumped onto the grass below, trying to escape the blaze. They appeared to survive the fall but were hurt.

"This is a nightmare!" a nurse screamed before attempting to use CPR to resuscitate a young woman who'd been dragged out of the building unconscious.

The sprinkler system at Everglades hadn't worked in years. A work order had been placed with the state three years prior. Even though a patient had set fire to the hospital twice before, the powers that be took their sweet time doing anything. Now it was too late.

CHAPTER TWO

Ebony Knight slumped down low in the seat of the stolen pickup truck that she was driving as she made a swift exit from the parking lot of Everglades Psychiatric Hospital. She passed a fire truck on its way to extinguish the blaze and glanced in the rearview mirror. The building was engulfed in flames. When she and her roommate, Kira, had set the fire, they'd only wanted a distraction big enough to cover their escape, but from the looks of things, their plan had gone awry. An ambulance whizzed past her. People were probably hurt, but she shook the thought off. She had to focus on her goal: revenge.

The mental hospital was located deep within the Florida Everglades, and Ebony had no idea where she was going, but her instincts told her to turn in the opposite direction from where the trucks were coming. Paranoid, she glanced in the rearview again, and this time she swore she saw Kira, running in the heavily wooded area on the side of the road.

Ebony rubbed her eyes. They had to be irritated by the smoke. What she'd seen had to have been a deer or some other kind of animal. There was no way she'd seen Kira. After they'd started the fire, Kira seemed hypnotized by the flames, and just as they were about to make their escape to the getaway vehicle, Ebony saw Kira run back into the burning building screaming some gibberish about returning to "the nebula," her imaginary home planet of Funkanova. Ebony couldn't stop her.

A part of Ebony regretted working with Kira to escape. Kira was unstable at best, and Ebony should have known that any plan she hatched would have disastrous results, but when it came to escaping, Ebony felt that she didn't have a choice. No way was she going to sit patiently and wait to be released from a mental hospital she shouldn't have been in. She'd been set up, and no way in hell was Ebony going to let the woman who'd destroyed her life get away with her crimes.

Ebony had to get out of Everglades, and Kira had offered a solution. Setting a fire and faking their deaths had been her idea. Ebony had been so blinded by rage that she went along. But Kira and Ebony didn't discuss what to do after the escape, and Ebony didn't know what her next moves were going to be.

Ebony stopped at the first gas station she came across—a practically deserted truck stop—and cut the engine on the truck. She had a full tank of gas but needed to pee and to at least splash some water on her face before she continued on her journey. She switched on the interior light and looked at herself in the mirror attached to the back of the sun visor. Her face and white wifebeater were covered with soot and ash. She rummaged through the glove compartment and side compartments in search of a napkin. She didn't find any napkins but did find a leather wallet with a $20 bill inside. Ebony slipped the money in her pocket.

She entered the gas station convinced that everyone was staring at her. She was right. Only three or four people were in the station, all white, all not used to seeing many black people in their neck of the woods, especially not dirty and disheveled black women. Ebony moved swiftly, grabbing a bottle of water and a POWERAde. She looked at the wrinkled, rubbery hot dogs rotating on metal warming cylinders, and although she wouldn't normally ingest such a disgusting sight, she fixed two franks and grabbed a handful of napkins. She put her things on the counter, where a female clerk looked at her with disdain.

"Got any scissors?" Ebony asked.

"Right over there." The clerk pointed at a small display of school supplies, never taking her eyes off Ebony.

"How about peroxide?" Ebony asked, smiling.

"Maybe. If there is any, it's over there by the Band-Aids and feminine products." The clerk continued to stare.

Ebony grabbed a pair of scissors and a bottle of peroxide, then picked up a Florida T-shirt that was in a bin marked $5.

"You all right?" the clerk asked, eyeing Ebony suspiciously. "You look like you've been in a fight or something."

"I'm fine. Just had a long day riding ATVs," Ebony lied smoothly. "I fell off but I'll be okay. Thanks for asking."

Ebony handed her the $20 bill and got $3 and some change back. She dipped out of the station as quickly as she could without breaking into a full-out run and got into the truck. She'd just have to relieve her bladder later. Ebony practically inhaled the hot dogs, greedily licking the mustard and ketchup off her dirty fingers as she drove back onto the dark road. She traveled until she reached a motel. She didn't have enough money to get a room, so she simply parked in the lot. She stood next to the truck in the darkness, pulled down her pants, and squatted awkwardly. Then she yanked up her pants and curled up in the back of the cab to get some rest.

"Your prick was so small I couldn't even feel it. Thanks for the easy fifty dollars!" Ebony heard a woman yell loudly. It seemed as if she'd only been asleep an hour, but the sun was rising. She looked at the clock on the dashboard: 4:49. Ebony sat up to see a hooker walking out of a motel room, still adjusting her revealing and tacky clothing. Her john turned beet red and scurried away to a rusted station wagon, and the pro headed off toward a trailer park across the road. They'd left the door to the motel room slightly ajar. It was just the break she needed. Ebony jumped out of the truck and rushed inside.

She locked the door, put the safety latch on, and worked with lightning speed. She stripped out of her filthy hospital-issued clothes. Standing naked in front of a dirty mirror, Ebony ran her fingers through her hair.

Thick, pretty, long hair, just like Mama's, she thought, admiring the soft waves full of natural body. Ebony choked back tears as she thought back to a time when she was thirteen and she'd tried to trim her ends. She'd only intended to take off about half an inch and did such a poor job that to correct it her mother had to cut off four inches.

"A woman's hair is her crowning glory, especially when it's so long like ours. Women pay good money to have hair like this, so don't you ever cut it again, you hear me?" Her mother cried as she cut her daughter's hair. Ebony had kept that promise for a dozen years.

"I'm sorry, Mama," Ebony now said softly. "I'm so, so sorry. All of this is my fault. If I had just listened to you about Carmelita, none of this would have happened. You never trusted her. I might not have gotten rich, but all the money in the world can't bring you back to me. Oh, God! What have I done? What am I doing? I just, I just don't know. I was so fucking greedy and stupid!" Ebony yelled, and banged her reflection in the mirror with her fist.

Angrily she took the pair of scissors she'd purchased and hacked at her waist-length hair. With every snip Ebony felt a bit weaker, a bit more confused, but she kept cutting until all that remained was a chin-length bob with bangs that covered her eyes.

It'll grow back, she told herself. *And then I'll never cut it again. I swear, Mama.*

Ebony took a shower and cried as she washed her hair

15

with the cheap motel shampoo and scrubbed her dirty body. Her body shook from the force of her sobs. Her mind whirled as she remembered her mother, how hard she'd struggled and all the things they'd gone through just to survive. She remembered when her mother hustled bricks of cocaine and how she'd got caught because of a low-down informant. Ebony remembered how she and her mother were arrested and questioned, and how they ultimately conspired to kill the informant; Ebony lured the informant into a hotel room with the promise of sex but slipped him a toxic dose of cocaine.

Knowing that a man died at her hands made Ebony numb and cold, and it took a long time for her to regain any sense of warmth. Just when everything seemed to be normalizing, when Ebony had gained financial security for her mother and herself and she was going to get married—it all fell apart. Ebony could feel the chill of indifference for the world and everyone in it creeping over her once more. She knew that she'd never be the same.

Ebony poured the bottle of peroxide over her head, then used the blow-dryer that was chained to the wall in an attempt to accelerate the bleaching of her hair. The change in color was subtle and a bit brassy but would have to do. Finally, she put on her old khakis and the Miami tourist T-shirt she'd picked up at the truck stop and exited the room. She hopped back in the truck and headed east, back toward Miami. She had a score to settle with an old friend, and plan or no plan, nothing but God Almighty was going to stop her.

CHAPTER THREE

Florida Everglades

A petite young woman sat on the ground at the side of a deserted road that ran through an area of swampland west of Miami. She'd been sitting for what felt like an eternity, being eaten alive by mosquitoes and paranoid that a gator or a snake was going to attack her. In the distance she finally saw headlights and stood quickly, running into the middle of the road. Her white T-shirt was nearly transparent with sweat and tied tightly just below her bosom, revealing a taut, firm young stomach. The khaki cutoff shorts she wore hugged her perky bottom. She wiggled sensually as she stuck out her thumb in an attempt to entice the oncoming vehicle to stop.

A truck with a plumbing-company logo emblazoned on its side pulled over. A man with badly sunburned skin and yellow teeth smiled at the woman.

He's disgusting, she said to herself.

"Where ya headed, honey?" the beefy driver asked, licking his lips.

"Wherever you want to take me," the woman said with a fake smile and a wink.

"Oh, I'll take you on a ride, honey," he said suggestively. "Get in."

The woman got in, the driver's eyes planted on her boobs as she pulled the seat belt across her chest.

"Well, let's ride," she said, smiling. She knew he was checking her out. She scanned the cab of the truck and gave the driver the once-over. He wore a cowboy hat and a belt with an outlandish buckle. The woman took notice of the shiny brass handle of a pocketknife peeking from a leather case attached to his belt. She swallowed hard. Her throat felt scratchy and beads of sweat began to form at her temples.

"What's your name?" he asked.

"Kira."

"That's pretty, just like you."

"Uh, thanks." Kira didn't want to know the driver's name. It would make what she knew she was going to have to do to him easier if she didn't know his name.

"Hot night tonight, huh?" she asked cheerfully, changing the direction of the conversation.

"Say, you a working girl or something?" the trucker asked, ignoring her question.

Kira looked the driver up and down. A rise in the crotch of his pants showed he was aroused. She rolled her eyes, then smiled. She knew it was going to come to this.

"I like to party but I'm not a pro. I just need a ride into the next town. I'd be ever so grateful," she said sweetly.

"Well, I'm headed toward Miami. Got a drop-off in Sweetwater. You can thank me for the ride at a little motel when we get there. Or you can start to thank me now as I drive."

The driver reached over and grabbed Kira's hand, moving it toward his erection. Kira recoiled and laughed.

"You know, there was a *chupacabra* in Sweetwater," she said, her eyes wide.

"A what?"

"A *chupacabra*. It means 'goat-sucker' in Spanish. It's a beast that feasts on the blood of animals, but they are known to feed on people. They mostly live in Latin America, but they're here, too."

"Little lady, ain't no such thing. Ain't no *chupacabbie* or whatever you said any more than there's a Sasquatch, bigfoot, or a Loch Ness monster."

"Oh, no, they're very real. Actually, I'm descended from a line of women who were raped by *chupacabras,*" Kira said matter-of-factly.

The trucker shot a curious glance at Kira.

"They escaped with their half-breed beast babies to the faraway planet of Funkanova, where pink reigns supreme." Kira grinned wildly, her eyes glazing over.

"Say what?" The driver had picked up many a hitchhiker in his day and had managed not to connect with any whack jobs. He hoped his luck hadn't changed.

"Funkanova, baby baby! All hail pink power!" Kira pumped her fist in the air.

"What the fuck? Hey, look, lady, I don't want no trouble."

"Oh, but you got it. You had it the minute that you took a job in Sweetwater. If you go there, the *chupacabra* is gonna get you. Hell, I might even morph and then you'll really be in trouble."

"Because I'm a gentleman I'm gonna pull over and let you out at the next gas station instead of putting you out in the middle of nowhere. But you have got to go."

"The hell you are!" Kira shouted. "I'm on my way to Miami and you're taking me. I can protect you with my lotus. I'll give it to you when we get there, but no Sweetwater!"

The driver ignored her.

"You do want to *do* me, don't you? C'mon, you know you want to. You would never turn down the chance to fuck a hot young thing like me. I'm buck wild, too. Ooh, yeah, baby." Kira began massaging her breasts and moaning, tossing her hair back and forth.

"Normally I'd jump at the chance, but my gut is telling me that you gotta go."

"You don't understand. I need revenge. Just like the *chupacabra,* my bloodthirst can not be satisfied! *Chupacabra!*" she yelled before leaning in toward the driver and biting his neck hard. The driver yelped in pain as the truck swerved violently. He recovered and pulled onto the gravel-covered shoulder of the road.

"Get the fuck out!" he yelled. He was about to back-slap her when he felt a searing pain in his belly. He looked down to see blood spreading in a maroon circle across his white T-shirt. The bitch had stabbed him with his own knife. Before he could react, she stabbed him again and again and again.

Kira's hands were covered in blood. She stared at them for a while, her breathing becoming more rapid as she watched the crimson droplets roll toward her wrists. She brought a hand to her face and inhaled, then she licked the blood from her pinkie. Her pointed tongue flickered over her delicate hand, lapping up the blood as she grunted. Kira's body tensed and she let out a loud moan of ecstasy. She always came when she satisfied her bloodthirst.

"You should be thanking me, you know. If I hadn't killed you, the *chupacabra* would have," Kira said, looking over at the driver. "Now I know that no one likes to be stabbed in the gut. It's a horrible way to go. A knife piercing your lungs, your liver, your kidneys, and such has got to be painful. But imagine the pain of a goat-monster ripping out your intestines and entrails and feasting on them. A goat-monster with cloven hooves, I might add, so you know he's evil. That's got to be the absolute worst way I can think of to go. That and fire!"

Kira held the dead trucker's face in her hands and stroked his hair. His eyes were rolled back, the milky whites showing. She leaned over and cut the engine on the truck, then began to search the man's pockets. She pulled out his wallet and looked inside. There were a couple hundred in cash, a credit card, and a gas card. *Sweet!*

Kira exited the truck, and with a strength that belied her petite frame, she dragged the bloody corpse over to the passenger side. Then she hopped into the driver's seat.

"See the thing is, you should have been more careful where you picked up a hitchhiker. It was pretty stupid to do that near a mental hospital." Kira looked over at the corpse and smiled. "My roommate and I did it, you know. We pulled it off! The old fakerooni! We started the fire so we could escape, and I bet everyone thinks we're dead. I bet that even Ebony thinks that I'm dead. I ran back to the building, but I didn't run back inside. I just had to see my masterpiece up close. Man, we burned that bitch up! It was so beautiful. I can't explain it. It was like Christmas and the Fourth of July all rolled into one. The roof, the roof, the roof was on fire! We ain't need no water, we let the motherfucker burn!"

Kira laughed and laughed.

"I did you a favor. Now you've got to do me one. I need a place to stay and I'll be needing supplies. You don't expect me to satisfy my bloodthirst without supplies, do you? No way, José. But I'm sure you have everything I need." She wiped off a streak of blood on the man's driver's license with her T-shirt and took off.

Almost an hour later Kira pulled into the carport of a dilapidated house. She looked around. There was a parked classic Thunderbird and a utility shed with a flimsy lock. She searched in the darkness for something to help her and saw a rusted toolbox. She opened it and found that it contained little more than a bent screwdriver, a wrench, and some rusty nails, but that was all she would need. Working fastidiously, she slipped the screwdriver into the crack of the door and banged on the handle with the wrench. She pried on the door until the flimsy wood planks of the shed door cracked and broke. Kira opened the shed, smiled at the contents within, then let herself inside his home.

The trucker's house smelled musty, and empty pizza boxes and beer cans were strewn about. She headed into the kitchen and rummaged through the drawers and cabinets. Again she smiled at the contents. There were plenty of knives, lighters, matches, and, most important, flammable liquids. There was everything she'd need for a successful bloodthirst.

Kira peeled her clothes off and walked stark naked into the bathroom. She turned on the water in the dirty shower and stepped inside. The water ran light pink as it washed traces of blood off her body and down the drain. Kira hummed happily to herself as she washed her hair. Then she turned off the water and, not bothering to dry herself off, moved into the bedroom. The bed was unmade and the sheets looked dirty, but she was tired. She searched for something to sleep in, but all the trucker's clothes looked dirtier than the sheets. Kira yanked the sheets off the mattress, but it was stained.

What a fucking slob, she thought. But she'd slept on worse at Everglades. Kira lay down and quickly drifted off to sleep. She would continue her quest after she rested.

When Kira woke up naked in a strange bed, she was at first disoriented. Then she began to remember what she'd done. She'd killed a truck driver and made her way to Miami. She'd officially begun her bloodthirst, and the very thought of it sexually excited her. She began to rub between her legs roughly, biting her lip as she masturbated to a quick orgasm.

"I must have more," she said aloud after she came. "Once I complete my mission, I can return to the nebula."

Kira stretched and got out of bed. She put on her dirty clothes and rummaged through the trucker's drawers and his closet. She knew a guy like him had to have a gun somewhere, and she was right. She found an old hunting rifle and a box of ammunition in the closet and smiled as she put them in a navy blue duffel bag she found there as well. Then she headed into the kitchen.

Kira collected the sharpest and biggest knives she could find and put them in the duffel bag, then she gathered every aerosol can she could find and placed them on top of the stove. She gathered all the bottles of cleaning supplies she could find and opened them, pouring them in a trail toward the door that led to the carport.

Next, Kira grabbed a couple of dirty kitchen cloths and tied them together. She turned the gas on the stove on and carried a bag of garbage into the doorway and let it sit in the puddle of mixed cleaning supplies that she created before walking out of the house.

She pulled out the trucker's keys and got into the Thunderbird, then cranked the engine. She pulled out of the driveway and let the car run near the curb. Kira ran up to the plumbing truck and peeked in the window. She saw the dead man's bloody corpse and began to laugh, then opened the gas tank and stuck the rope of kitchen cloths she'd tied together inside the tank. Kira turned the makeshift rope around and inserted the clean end and let the end that had been doused in gasoline dangle outside the tank, careful not to get any gas on her hands. Then she walked to the shed, pulled out a machete, and headed to the bag of garbage in the home's doorway.

Kira lit the bag of garbage and moved quickly to the truck, igniting the rope hanging from the gas tank before running to the idling Thunderbird. She stood momentarily dazed, humming softly to herself as she waited for the gas fumes to meet the burning garbage and explode. When they did, the blast wasn't as intense as she would have liked, but it was satisfying enough for her to get inside the car and drive away, cackling as she watched the truck blow up moments after the house in the rearview mirror.

CHAPTER FOUR

Hialeah, Florida

Ebony Knight sat on an old stool with a cracked vinyl seat in a Hialeah café, awaiting a cup of Cuban coffee. She was exhausted and her body ached thanks to the uncomfortable nap she'd taken in the stolen truck. For an instant she wished she'd got at least a couple hours of sleep in the motel where she'd undergone her makeover, but she knew she had to stay mobile, at least for the time being. She was a fugitive, a target, and a moving target was harder to hit.

The waitress slid a demitasse of Bustelo across the counter. As soon as the thick liquid's pungent aroma hit her nostrils, Ebony felt a jolt of energy course through her system. Her senses reawakened, she thought about the path that lay ahead of her. Getting revenge without getting caught wasn't going to be easy. Carmelita was wily and cunning and wouldn't go down without a fight, but Ebony was just as smart, and not only was she willing to fight, she was willing to die to fulfill her vendetta.

A news report about the fire at Everglades played on a tiny television perched on a stand behind the counter.

"Por favor, sube el volumen." Ebony asked the waitress to turn up the volume.

When she did, Ebony leaned forward and watched the story.

"A devastating fire took the lives of two patients and a guard at Everglades Psychiatric Hospital here in the Florida Everglades about thirty miles west of Miami-Dade County. The fire department isn't sure how the blaze started, but one of the deceased patients, Kira Long, is a known arsonist. The other patient presumed dead in the fire is Ebony Knight. Ms. Knight was recently cleared of murder charges of the powerful South Florida businessman and philanthropist Erik Johansen and beloved Cuban-American photographer Jeff Cardoza, but was ordered to stay in the psychiatric facility to receive treatment for an unknown illness. Also dead in the fire is security guard Rudolph Jenkins."

Marisol Rivera-Frye, a pretty Cuban-American reporter, stood in front of the burned-down carcass of Everglades Psychiatric Hospital holding a microphone. Next to her stood a woman practically bawling her eyes out.

"But that isn't where this tragic but intriguing story ends," Marisol continued dramatically. "I'm here with one of Ebony Knight's doctors in Everglades, Dr. St. John."

"This is truly a loss," Dr. St. John said to Marisol. "Ebony Knight was not the woman people thought that she was. She was truly misunderstood and, unfortunately, misdiagnosed. I was about to recommend her for release, and I believe it would have been granted. I just didn't get to do it in time," the doctor said, teary-eyed. She covered her face with one hand. "I'm sorry, but I can't do this right now."

"And there you have it. A visibly shaken staff member at Everglades Psychiatric Hospital reacting to the death of one of the patients, Ebony Knight, who was cleared of murder charges and was believed by her doctor to have been ready for release but was killed before that could happen. We'll bring you more updates as coverage of this story continues. For WSVN, Channel Seven, I'm Marisol Rivera-Frye, reporting."

Ebony rolled her eyes in disgust at the sight of her doctor from that hellish mental institution, blubbering and carrying on with a reporter as if she were so broken up.

A lot of help all that crying is doing now, Dr. St. John, she thought sarcastically. *You should have listened to me in the first place, you quack! Things wouldn't have had to end this way.*

Ebony got up and went to the restroom. After splashing some water on her face, she exited the café. Her first stop was South Miami, where she kept a safe-deposit box. She planned on being the first person there when the doors opened at 9 a.m. In the box was $20,000 in cash along with a couple of charge cards, an extra set of house keys, and some paperwork pertaining to her home and businesses. She was grateful that she'd got it in case of an emergency, such as a fire or a hurricane. She was even more grateful that she had got it anonymously at a personal storage center and not through her bank.

Once there, accessing the box was a breeze. She simply wrote a passcode on a slip of paper and was given a key, then a man walked with her through a series of heavy-duty doors and a maze of vaults. He used his master key to unlock one lock, and Ebony used her key to unlock the other. Then he removed the metal box storing Ebony's possessions and escorted her into a private room.

After the door closed, she opened her box. A wave of relief washed over her as she pulled out the old, black, oversize Coach bag she'd stashed the items in. Ebony looked inside and smiled. The money was there, bundled in rubber bands, and the papers were in manila envelopes. She extracted her spare house keys and put them in her pocket along with a couple hundred dollars, then she closed the bag and kept it moving.

Ebony drove to Marshalls to pick up some discounted clothes. She didn't want anything extravagant or eye-catching, just survival gear: a basic pair of lightweight cotton pants, a pair of denim shorts, a plain cotton tank, a plain cotton shirt, a pair of gym shoes, some sunglasses, and a few bra-and-panty sets. Ebony felt her chest tighten and it became harder to breathe as she moved swiftly through the racks of marked-down clothing. Every time someone made eye contact with her, it felt as if the person knew who she was. She fidgeted and her hands shook as she paid for her purchases, and she was convinced that a SWAT team would surround her the minute she exited the store. Ebony knew she had to get off the street and go somewhere she could get her mind right.

As she drove north on U.S. 1, she tried to remain focused, but so many thoughts were swirling through her head, and panic and fear were clouding her judgment. When she'd first embarked on her vendetta, she was driven by pure anger and hatred, but as time wore on, reality began to set in. There was no more denying the truth. If she didn't have a solid plan, she could plan on failing, and failure was not an option.

Ebony had to do some reconnaissance. She had to pinpoint Carmelita's location; she could be staying in her own condo, she could be living in Ebony's home, or she could have taken everything and fled halfway across the globe. Getting a hold on Carmelita wasn't a difficult task for a smart and resourceful woman like Ebony, but it meant that she needed to get connected. She didn't have a cell phone or a computer, two things that had once been like extensions of herself, but if she could get them, it would make getting the information she needed much easier. Her first thoughts were of a PDA, but she'd need ID to get a decent cell phone with internet access, and the flea markets where she could come up on a bootleg weren't open during the week.

She figured a television, radio, and landline would have to do, but Ebony didn't plan on posting up anywhere for any length of time. Time was of the essence; she had to act quickly. She was presumed dead, but for how long? How long would it take for Carmelita to legally claim Ebony's estate as her own? Ebony had no living relatives, and Carmelita had been named her conservator. It appeared that Carmelita had nothing standing in her path.

Ebony headed toward the hood. Although before being committed to Everglades she had lived in the lap of luxury, Ebony never forgot her roots. She knew of a motel off the expressway, down the street from Coco's and the Lexxx strip clubs, where she could stay on the cheap but, more important, without having to show a driver's license or ID.

Ebony also knew she had to get rid of the bright red truck she was driving. The tags were registered to a dead man, and when it was discovered that the truck was missing, the police would start putting two and two together. But she couldn't just abandon it; it had her prints and probably hair all over it. She wasn't about to try to clean it herself. She'd watched enough *CSI* to know that she'd miss something that the cops would find.

What she needed to do was find a chop shop, but she had no idea how to go about doing it. The whole point of a chop shop was that it was secret; people didn't advertise that sort of business.

Ebony spotted a corner store and decided to go inside to pick up some necessities before she hit the motel. She put on her shades and looked in the rearview mirror. No one would recognize her with short hair, she told herself. She looked like an entirely different person. Ebony went inside. She grabbed a few toiletries, some snacks, a bottle of Coke, and two twenty-four-ounce bottles of Heineken, then stood in line to buy them and a box of Newports.

The guy ahead of her turned around to face her while he waited for the cashier to give him his change.

"Damn, girl, you fine as hell," he said with a wide smile that revealed a row of gold teeth. He couldn't have been more than eighteen or nineteen years old. He would actually have been a young cutie if he hadn't destroyed his look with tacky gold fronts. Ebony didn't want to give him even the slightest glimmer of hope that she'd talk to him. She simply nodded.

"You can't say thank you?" the young man asked.

"Thanks," Ebony replied drily as the young man's eyes roamed over her body. Ebony rolled her eyes and stepped up to the counter.

"You are a very pretty girl," the clerk said in a heavy Hindu accent. "Very sexy."

"Mmm-hmm," Ebony hummed, barely acknowledging him. As she reached to get her change, the clerk attempted to stroke her hand with his fingertips. Ebony snatched her hand back and stalked out of the store, muttering to herself angrily, *Fucking men! They act like they've never seen a woman before! I am not in the mood for all of this!*

The young man who'd tried to pick her up inside was waiting for her by the truck. "Who that other Heineken for?"

Ebony didn't answer; she walked to the driver's side of the truck and let herself in.

"Why you gotta be like that, baby?" he asked, grinning and following her. Ebony rolled down her window.

"Do not follow me like that," she growled at him.

"You ain't gotta be so mean, girl," the man said, continuing to flirt.

"What is it with you men? Can't you tell when a woman doesn't want to be bothered?" Ebony snapped. She was going to get the hell out of Dodge, but just as she was about to throw the truck into gear, she heard a series of loud pops she instantly recognized as gunfire. She instinctively ducked down. When she sat back up, Ebony felt something cold hit her temple. She froze.

"Move over!" The young buck who'd been flirting with her was holding a gun to her head. He yanked the truck door open. She thought about the security guard's gun she'd found earlier, which was stashed in the glove compartment. She wouldn't be able to reach it before she got blasted. Ebony held her hands in the air and squeezed her eyes shut as she moved over into the passenger side as quickly as she could.

Ebony felt the truck take off and heard the tires squeal on the concrete. Gunshots ricocheted off the body of the truck. Glass from the rear window flew everywhere as a bullet blew through it and whizzed above her head, before blowing out the front windshield.

"Oh my God!" she shrieked as the truck spun out of control.

She gripped the handle on the door, closed her eyes, and clenched her teeth, bracing for impact. It didn't come. She opened her eyes and looked around. The truck had barely missed hitting an SUV. People were standing in the street pointing at the truck. She turned toward the young man that had jacked her. He was brushing glass off his shirt and shaking out his dreadlocks. Ebony's eyes flitted about frantically, searching for his gun. It had fallen onto the floor during their spin-out. She made a move for the glove compartment.

"Don't even think about it!" the jacker warned, using his forearm to slam Ebony back into her seat. Ebony bit his arm, causing him to jump in surprise. She seized the moment, leaning forward and opening the glove compartment, snatching the handgun stowed inside. But she wasn't quick enough. By the time she turned to aim the gun at the carjacker, he'd recovered his gun and was aiming it at her.

"Wait a minute!" Ebony screamed with the gun in one hand, her other hand in the air in surrender. He didn't make a move. Ebony's heart was racing like NAS-CAR. "Look, I don't know how the fuck you went from trying to holla at me to trying to kill me, but I don't want any trouble."

"Then put your fucking gun down."

"I'm not putting my gun down," Ebony said sternly. "Not until I know exactly what the fuck is going on."

"I'm not putting mine down. And I'm not much for conversation." He pulled the hammer back on his pistol.

The look in his eyes told Ebony that he'd have no prob-lem shooting her, shoving her body out of the car, and rolling over it.

"Please," she begged, quickly putting the gun down on the seat between them. "It doesn't have to get ugly. You can have this truck, just let me out. I swear I won't say shit."

"I don't need or want this fucking truck."

"What is it that you want me to do then?"

In the distance there was the wail of police sirens. The driver looked nervous and so did Ebony.

"Don't be stupid. The police are coming. Let me out, take the truck, and get out of here!" Ebony screamed frantically.

"Hell no! If I let you out, your ass is gonna run straight to the police."

"No, I promise I won't," Ebony said quickly.

"That's bullshit," he said, brushing glass off his shoul-ders.

"I swear I won't. I can't. It's a really long story, but to sum it up, me and the police aren't on the best of terms. Plus, this truck is stolen. Neither one of us wants to get caught in it. The police are the last people I want to run into."

"I can't take that chance," young dreadlocks said. The sirens were getting louder and closer.

"Fine, but we gotta get out of here," Ebony said. "Now! Or it's both our asses!"

The dread looked at Ebony through squinted eyes.

He put his gun down in the waistband of his pants and sped off.

"What just happened back there?" Ebony asked the dread as they flew through the Miami streets. "Who was shooting at you?"

"Don't worry about it." He swerved and maneuvered around a sharp corner.

"I almost got shot back there myself because you were standing there talking to me when I didn't want to be bothered, so don't tell me not to worry about it," Ebony snapped.

The young man said nothing.

"Where are we going?"

"Just be quiet," he said angrily. "I need to think."

"Look, we cool right? You're gonna let me out somewhere, right?"

"Didn't you hear me tell you to be quiet?" he barked.

Ebony sucked her teeth and shifted her eyes to the side mirror to check for the police. None were coming.

"I think we shook them," Ebony told her captor, breathing a sigh of relief.

"Of course I shook them. The po-pos ain't no match for me."

"You run from the police often?" Ebony asked sarcastically.

"It's better than being caught by them." He was twisting and turning through side streets.

"What's even better is to not have the police after you at all," Ebony replied with a smirk.

"Whatever."

"So, are you at least going to tell me your name?"

"What does it matter?"

"After all this I could at least know your name."

He didn't respond.

"I can't believe this," Ebony muttered under her breath. *Maybe this is God's way of trying to stop me from doing something crazy. Or maybe it's just a crazy coincidence.* Ebony ran her hands through her hair and exhaled. She resolved to remain steadfast in her mission to get Carmelita and was determined to carry out her plan.

"Did you hear me?" the man asked.

Ebony looked up. "Did you say something?"

"I said that we're gonna make a stop and have someone come get this truck."

"And *then* I can leave, right?"

"And then we'll see" was all he said.

Ebony didn't like his answer, nor the way his eyes roamed over her body when he said it, but she knew whatever this stranger had in store for her she could handle. *For your sake, your intentions better be honorable. Or you can add your name to my death list.*

CHAPTER FIVE

After reporter **Marisol** Rivera-Frye finished her interview with Everglades Psychiatric Hospital psychiatrist Dr. St. John, she and her cameraman walked around getting more shots of the burned-down carcass of the building and interviews with fire department officials still on the scene and employees unaware of the fire who had reported to work. Marisol noticed Dr. St. John walking around the rubble where the facility once stood. Marisol couldn't tell whether the doctor was praying or meditating, but she'd been there for nearly an hour before Marisol finally walked over to her and tapped her on the shoulder.

"Dr. St. John, I know this isn't a good time, but I've got to ask you, off the record if you like, did Everglades have an active safety environment?"

"I don't know what you mean."

"I mean it seems to me that a lot of people died needlessly today."

"Look, I understand that you have a job to do, but don't you have any tact? Can't you see that I'm upset?"

Dr. St. John wiped her eyes. "I can't answer your questions right now. Maybe it was a mistake agreeing to talk to you."

"I see that you're very upset. A great tragedy occurred here. I'm not trying to be coldhearted by downplaying that, but I find it odd that you're so . . . emotional about the death of two mental patients and a security guard."

"I care a great deal about my patients and colleagues!"

"Well, I'm sure you do, but I don't believe that the tears you're crying are for Ebony Knight, Kira Long, or Rudolph Jenkins."

"Excuse me?" Dr. St. John asked, not making any attempt to hide her anger.

"Let me make myself more clear. You look like you feel guilty, not sad. After all, you admitted yourself that you'd made a misdiagnosis. And maybe you know where the money that should have gone toward fixing the hospital's safety violations was really going. Perhaps you even had a hand in the cookie jar."

"I'm not going to listen to this."

"The taxpayers of this state have a right to know what's going on here. Their money pays for state-run institutions like Everglades. Why didn't you and the other members of the hospital's administration do something? Is it because you were too busy cashing your fat checks to care? Don't you think you owe it to the families of the victims to talk about what you know? Don't you think that people with loved ones in state care deserve to know if they're being properly cared for? And speaking of proper care, how many other misdiagnoses aside from Ebony Knight have you made? Don't you feel a sense of personal responsibility? Do you ask yourself if you hadn't been careless, would Ebony Knight still be alive?" Marisol cocked an eyebrow at Dr. St. John and stood with her hands on her hips.

"I don't have to answer to you."

"No, you don't. But it would make things easier. I'd hate to have to dig and pry into your record and discover how many other patients you've misdiagnosed. I mean, there could be sane people locked up and crazy people running free all over South Florida. The government hires you for forensic psychiatry. They consider you an expert. Imagine how tainted your reputation could be after a scathing exposé by yours truly. And imagine the damage to your reputation if it comes out that your BMW was paid for by the money that should have gone to the hospital." Marisol pointed at Dr. St. John's BMW 745.

"Are you threatening me, Marisol Rivera-Frye? Because I don't scare easily. As a psychiatrist I've dealt with people far more clever than the likes of you. I won't be a part of your dirty journalism. Do what you have to do," Dr. St. John said, breezing past Marisol and getting into her car.

Marisol Rivera-Frye smiled and walked to the news truck. *You're covering something up, Dr. St. John, and I'm going to figure out what it is.*

★ ★ ★

Dr. St. John grabbed the steering wheel of her beamer until her knuckles were white. She let out a frustrated scream and banged her fist on the dashboard before turning her CD player up as loud as it would go. The sounds of Metallica singing "Enter Sandman" blared so loud that her ears rang. Dr. St. John uttered a string of vulgarities, then calmly turned down the volume on the stereo and took some deep, meditative breaths.

Don't let her get to you, she told herself. *That reporter is just a busybody out for a story. She was trying to rile you up for a sound bite.* But no matter what Dr. St. John said to make herself feel better, it didn't change that Marisol Rivera-Frye had a point. She *did* feel guilty for knowing what a horrible condition the hospital was in and not making more of a fuss about things. And she *did* feel personally responsible for Ebony Knight's demise.

Ebony had told her that her being in Everglades was a mistake, that she wasn't mentally ill. She'd also told her that her mother was in danger, but Dr. St. John didn't pay attention to Ebony's pleas for help until it was too late. The truth was, Dr. St. John treated Ebony just like any other patient that she saw, with casual disregard and disinterest, covered with the veneer that she was actually listening.

But Dr. St. John couldn't pay attention to every psychiatric patient who claimed to be "sane." Paranoid delusions, alternative realities, and dissociated personalities were all in a day's work for her. Yet somehow a truly sane person had slipped through the cracks and was lumped in with all the other "special people." And Dr. St. John hadn't known the difference. It all sounded typical of a paranoid schizophrenic. Besides, she could have done nothing to prevent the fire. She was a psychiatrist, not a psychic. Plus, on her own she could have done nothing to cut through all the bureaucratic red tape it would have taken to make sure the hospital was up to code.

There's nothing I could have done. Now all I can do is go forward in healing and put this all behind me, Dr. St. John told herself. She kept telling herself that until she actually believed it.

Rene Fields glared as Marisol Rivera-Frye breezed in and threw her purse and coat on top of Rene's desk as if she were the tyrannical boss from hell in *The Devil Wears Prada*. Rene hated working for Marisol, who was demanding, rude, and had no idea how to treat people. On top of that she wasn't very bright, but Marisol didn't seem to realize it. She thought she'd become the "Queen of Miami News" because of her talent and determination, but Rene knew better. Marisol was a ratings magnet not because of her hard-hitting investigatory skills, but because she was eye candy with a big rack, a model-turned-weathergirl-turned-reporter. Marisol was no journalist. On the other hand, Rene had graduated at the top of her J-school class.

But Rene knew a plum opportunity when she saw one. She was going to be a star reporter one day, but first she had to get her foot in the right door. Marisol's door was perfect. All Rene had to do was wait for the perfect time and she would waltz right in and show Marisol, the station's powers-that-be, and all of Miami how reporting the news was really done. Marisol's big mistake was that she thought she actually struck fear in Rene's heart; Marisol thought by being mean to Rene she was keeping her in her place. Marisol had no clue that her assistant didn't fear her one bit, didn't respect her, and that each time she treated Rene like garbage, she was keeping a tally, relishing that sooner rather than later it was going to be not only easy but pleasurable dethroning Marisol. She'd never see it coming.

"Stop everything that you're doing. I need you to get started on the research of my next exposé!" Marisol commanded. Rene temporarily forgave her boss's rudeness since it meant working on a juicy story.

"Let me guess. You're going to uncover the escape of the two patients from the mental hospital, right? The security guard is in on it, huh? I knew it!" Rene clapped her hands, then rubbed them together with excitement.

"What on earth are you babbling about, Rene?" Marisol rolled her eyes.

"The fire at Everglades? Ebony Knight . . ."

Marisol threw her head back and laughed. "Oh, Rene, you have such an imagination. Really, an escape by two mental patients? That's pretty far-fetched."

"How is it far-fetched? You talked to her psychiatrist this morning. Think about it. The doctor said that Ebony wasn't crazy. Now she, her roommate, and a security guard are the only ones presumed dead. Why was everyone else able to get out of the building but them? It's obvious they started the fire, and it's obvious they did it to escape."

"I don't find those things obvious at all. If their bodies or at least some charred remains aren't found, then I will go down that road. For now I'm not going to go chasing phantom stories. I'm going to focus on what's real and right in front of my face."

"Which is?" Rene asked, her voice thick with disappointment.

"The obvious neglect, malpractice, and disorganization at that hospital. The sprinklers didn't work. That whole fire could have been prevented with a few smoke detectors and the sprinkler system the law required them to have. I want to know why those safety precautions weren't in place. And the public has a right to know as well."

"Sure, Marisol," a deflated Rene said. "Just tell me what you need me to do."

"I need you to make phone calls, and lots of them, to city officials, reps from the fire department, the department of health and human services. Really egg them on so you can get really candid statements. Remember, the juicier the better. And see if you can get in touch with the security guard's widow. I'm sure she'll have something good to say."

"Is that all?" Rene asked, already bored with the task.

"Are you sure you don't need me to do some legwork? You know, help you out with some of the interviews you're going to use."

"No, I need you here. Also, find out all you can about Dr. Suzette St. John. She was Ebony's doctor at Everglades. I had the distinct feeling that she was covering something up during our interview this morning."

Yeah, like that she knows two psychos are on the loose, Rene thought.

"I'm telling you, Rene. This story has Emmy written all over it!" Marisol enthused.

It sure does. My Emmy. Once I uncover the truth that you're too blind to see, I will be the new queen, Rene vowed.

Carmelita Sanchez had been unable to focus since she'd heard the news that Everglades Psychiatric Hospital had burned to the ground. Her nemesis, Ebony Knight, was dead, or so it was being reported. If that was accurate, then Ebony's fortune was totally and legally hers. Not that it mattered. Carmelita had emptied Ebony's bank accounts long before the fire.

But what if she isn't dead? A niggling voice tugged at Carmelita's subconscious. *It's all so coincidental. Too coincidental!*

If Ebony Knight was alive, that could only mean one thing. She was coming for Carmelita. And she wouldn't stop coming for her until she got what she wanted. An eye for an eye. Carmelita shuddered at the thought.

She knew that Ebony had received the news of her mother's death. She'd had her assistant send the message to the hospital in order to push her over the edge. Ebony didn't have the mental toughness to survive losing every single person she cared about. Carmelita figured that Ebony would finally have a true breakdown and then her plan would be complete. Ebony Knight would no longer be a threat. Now Carmelita was worried. Maybe the news pushed Ebony *too far* over the edge. Far enough over to set fire to the hospital and escape to get revenge. After all, it was pretty odd that only three people were missing in the fire. It just didn't sit right with her.

Maybe you're feeling guilty because of all the things you did to her, Carmelita thought.

Carmelita shook the voice of her conscience out of her head. She had absolutely no reason to feel guilty about anything. Ebony had got what she deserved. If Ebony hadn't been weak, Carmelita wouldn't have had any reason to destroy her. Weakness was something Carmelita simply couldn't abide.

Ebony and Carmelita had recently pulled of the scam of the century. By blackmailing Erik Johansen they'd hit the jackpot. Then Ebony started to show Carmelita the chinks in her armor. The first sign of weakness that Ebony showed was her reluctance to sell the footage that could totally have destroyed Erik Johansen. Carmelita felt that blackmailing him with it should have been Ebony's first move, but Ebony felt sorry for the sick bastard and thought that cutting him off would be the best thing to do. Carmelita knew they were sitting on a gold mine, but no matter what she said, Ebony wouldn't budge.

It was a good thing that Erik didn't want to let Ebony go so easily. He almost pushed her to her limit, so Carmelita decided to nudge her over a cliff. She threw in a few eerie deliveries to Ebony and made it look as if Erik were the sender. She also cloned his cell phone and made tons of calls to Ebony using a voice-changing device the way the killer did in the movie *Scream*. Threatening to kill Ebony's fiancé that was the straw that broke her back.

Carmelita's phone rang.

"I've been calling you all morning! Where have you been?" a voice said hysterically before Carmelita even had a chance to say hello.

"Amber?" Carmelita asked. Amber had been Carmelita's lover off and on for a few years. They'd kept their relationship so low-profile Ebony didn't even know about it. It had to be that way for their scam to work, but Amber had been in with Carmelita every single step of the way in framing Ebony.

"Yes, it's me. Did you hear the news about Ebony?"

"I heard," Carmelita said coolly.

"Carm, how can you be so calm?"

"Look, I don't want any shit from you. Everything is under control." But that was all a front. Carmelita was far more panicked than she let on.

"But Ebony's doctor was on television saying that she knew that Ebony wasn't crazy. What else did she know? Maybe she knows that you killed Erik and Jeff?"

"Amber, you need to get a hold of yourself. There's nothing to worry about. The media is just sensational-izing things for ratings. This will all blow over once a bigger story breaks," Carmelita said, but she wasn't sure if she really believed that.

"I guess you're right. I trust you and your brilliant mind. Anyway, I can't believe she's really dead, baby. Now all that money is officially ours and we don't have to worry about any insanity hearings or her getting out of the crazy house."

"Ebony was *never* going to get out of Everglades. She was weak. I don't care if she was sane when she went in, there was no way she wouldn't *become* crazy being locked up like that. And even if she got released, she would have died before she got her hands on her money ever again because I would have killed her."

"I still don't understand why you did this. Why didn't you just let her get sent up the river? This was way too complicated."

"It was more fun this way," Carmelita replied, devoid of emotion.

"You're crazy, Carm, but that's why I love you. You're twisted, just like I am. I liked Ebony though. She was cool. Too bad it had to come to all of this."

"I'll talk to you later, Amber." Carmelita hung up.

The truth was, Carmelita liked Ebony, too. It was so disappointing to see how weak she really was. Things were going great until Ebony went and fell in love. She wanted to just walk away and get married despite that she could have got rich beyond her wildest dreams. Carmelita couldn't walk away from all that money. She wouldn't. Even if it meant betraying her best friend.

Carmelita knew in her heart that the secret she and Ebony shared would never truly be safe, even though Ebony would never snitch on her. At least not in the beginning. Although she tried to distance herself from them, Ebony still conducted herself according to the laws of the street, and those laws demanded silence. But those laws also demanded vengeance. Ebony wasn't going to let her get away with killing Jeff. Carmelita knew the shock would eventually wear off and Ebony would probably try to kill her. Or maybe she'd find religion and feel so guilt-ridden that she would tell the police who really committed the murders. In Carmelita's eyes there were too many what-ifs, and that meant too many chances for her plan to take over Ebony's life to fail. Carmelita couldn't let that happen, so she did the only thing she could do: strike hard, strike fast, and aim to totally destroy Ebony Knight.

Carmelita flipped through the Rolodex of business cards that sat on top of her desk until she found the one that she was looking for, then picked up the phone.

"Hi, this is Carmelita Sanchez. I need to plan a vacation to Europe."

Just in case, Carmelita thought as she made plans with her travel agent. *I've come too far for everything to fall apart now.*

CHAPTER SIX

Ebony and her captor arrived at a ranch–style, pale blue stucco house and pulled into the driveway. A row of mini–palm trees lined the walkway leading to the front porch, their huge fronds waving in the breeze.

"Come on," he said.

"Where are we?" Ebony asked.

"Girl, bring your ass on."

"Girl? I'm a grown-ass woman. The only child here is you. How old are you? Seventeen? Eighteen? Your ass should be in school instead of jacking women at the corner store."

"I'm a man. That's all you need to know. And I didn't jack you. Some dudes was after me and you were in the wrong place at the wrong time. You should be thanking me for getting you out of there." The young man opened the screen door and banged on a metal security door.

"Boy, you better stop banging on the door like you the damn police!" a heavyset woman with a Black & Mild cigarillo dangling between her lips snarled as she threw the door open. "What the fuck is going on?"

"Open the garage door," he said rudely, ignoring her.

"Who truck is this?"

"Mama, open the garage door please. Now!"

The woman sucked her teeth and shuffled to a side door. She opened it and reached her hand inside while keeping her eyes on Ebony.

"You're welcome," the woman said to her son sarcastically.

"Thanks," he grumbled.

"I don't know what you thinking. Just 'cause you got a lil' girl with you don't mean you can go getting new on me. I'm still the mama."

Ebony and her captor stepped inside the house.

"So who is you?" the woman asked Ebony, looking her up and down.

"Denise," she lied.

"I'm Miss Cat. You Nuquan's new girlfriend?"

"Nuquan?" Ebony stifled a giggle. *What the hell kind of name is Nuquan?*

"Stop grilling her, Ma." Nuquan had reentered the house through the garage.

"You done brought her up in my house, I can ask who she is if I want to," Miss Cat said, rolling her eyes and flipping her auburn-colored spiral curls over her shoulder.

"It's okay," Ebony said. "I'm not going to be staying long. As a matter of fact I was telling Nuquan that I had to be on my way. It was nice meeting you, Miss Cat." Ebony headed toward the door.

"Nah, you ain't going nowhere," Nuquan said with a menacing look. "Sit on the couch."

Ebony did as she was told, flopping down on a floral-print couch that was covered in plastic. Miss Cat smirked. "I don't know why any girl in her right mind would want to fuck with you, Nu-Nu. I swear you don't know how to treat a woman. Pretty as this girl is, you need to talk nice to her and be taking her someplace nice. Instead you got her in the middle of some shit. Is that bullet holes in that truck? Don't tell me you got this girl shot at while she was hanging out with you?"

Ebony bugged at how cavalier Miss Cat was; she made it seem as if Nuquan were always getting involved in shoot-outs.

"Mama, I'm hungry," Nuquan said, changing the subject. "You cook?"

"I ain't know we was having company," she said, cutting her eyes at Ebony. "But I was 'bout to fry some conch for lunch. I can throw some more in."

"Yeah, you go do that," Nuquan said. His mother went into the kitchen and turned the television up and began clanging pots and pans.

Disrespectful fucker, Ebony thought. *I would never have ordered my mama around like that.*

"You always talk to your mama like that?" Ebony asked Nuquan, turning up her nose in disapproval.

"You don't need to worry about me and my mama."

"Whatever. Let's handle our business then so I can go."

"What business would that be?"

Ebony sucked her teeth and frowned. "The business of

61

getting rid of that truck in the garage and then me getting the hell out of here."

"You just let me handle that."

"Wait a second. That's my truck."

"I thought you said it was stolen."

"It is. But I'm driving it, so it's mine now. Besides my
prints are in there, too, so I need to know what's up.
Ain't no just letting you handle things."

"You don't have a choice," Nuquan told her.

"Look, I don't know why people were shooting at
you, and frankly, now I don't care. If you're in some little
hood drama, then that's your own damned business. But
I'm in enough trouble and I'm not trying to be caught
in the middle of some more shit."

"What kind of trouble you in? And why was a girl
like you driving a stolen truck? I can tell you one of
them rich bitches."

"I'm not rich."

"Bullshit!" Nuquan smirked.

"Look at me. I ain't got on no flossy shit. Hello, I was
shopping at Marshalls. Do I look rich?" Ebony pointed
at her shopping bags.

"Nope, and that's how I can tell you rich. *Real* rich
folks like to dress down. I see that shit all the time. You
probably been working in your garden or something,"
Nuquan said in a mocking tone.

"I'm serious. I don't have a pot to piss in actually.
That's why I was in a stolen truck. I was on the come up."

"Who'd you steal it from?"

"None a," Ebony replied.

"You in the wrong spot to be talking slick. Don't get shit twisted. Just 'cause this is mama's house don't mean I won't kick your ass up in here."

Ebony gritted her teeth in anger. She knew she could go toe-to-toe with just about any man who didn't have a serious height advantage on her. After all, she'd made a living coming up with creative ways to inflict pain, but she didn't want to waste her energy battling a shorty named Nuquan. She had to get out of there and get to Carmelita.

"If I tell you, can I bounce?" Ebony asked.

"Yeah. Fuck it."

"Fine." She cleared her throat, thinking of a lie. "I ran a lick on this man I met on South Beach. I told him I was gonna party with him, and when he went into the gas station, I took off in his ride. I've been popped before and I'm on probation. I'm not trying to go back to jail."

"That's bullshit."

"That's real talk."

"You were partying on South Beach dressed like that?" Nuquan asked.

"That was last night. I just threw these clothes on to run errands."

"You're running errands in a stolen truck. Yeah, right. I don't believe you, but I'll play your little game. What were you going to do with the truck?"

"Chop it and pocket the money."

"You know somebody that can do that?"

"Maybe."

"You don't know shit," Nuquan said.

"Look, does it really matter how I got the truck? It's stolen. It's worth some money. You can have it all if you just let me go. I got some important shit to do."

"It's gonna have to wait. I'm about to go on and drink this other Heineken you bought, so I hope whoever you were taking it to wasn't thirsty." Nuquan popped the lid on the beer. Ebony glared at him. He popped the lid on the second beer and handed it to Ebony. "Drink your beer and calm down."

Nuquan and Ebony sat side by side on the couch with the television watching them. Nuquan was busy texting back and forth on his phone, and Ebony distracted herself by peeling the label off her Heineken.

"This is driving me crazy, Nuquan. Why am I just sitting here waiting? This is kidnapping, you know."

"Ain't nobody kidnapped your ass. I'm gonna let you go, I'm just waiting for shit to cool down. Trust me, I don't want to keep your ass. You talk too fucking much. Shit, you ain't feeling a buzz from that beer yet?" Nuquan asked, laughing. "Or maybe that's why you talking so much. Maybe you had too much beer."

"I'm straight. Are you? You probably aren't even old enough to be drinking that." Ebony crossed her arms.

"I'm old enough to do a lot of things. Want to find out what?"

"I don't think so."

"Your loss. Anyway, I got somebody coming over." He

shoved his phone in his pocket. "He's going to help me handle everything. In the meantime, I told you, relax."

"Whatever." Ebony picked at her fingernails, thinking she needed a manicure. In her former life she had been used to pampering herself with massages and spa treatments, but being on lockdown put an end to her princess lifestyle. *Soon,* she said silently. *Soon everything is going to be set right. I'll have my money and my revenge.*

"Nuquan, come here, boy!" Miss Cat shouted from the kitchen.

"I'm busy," he shouted back.

"I said come here! Now!"

"I'll be back. If you move, I'll kill you."

"All that extra shit isn't necessary," Ebony told him as he walked away. She could hear Nuquan and his mother talking but couldn't make out their words over the sound of the television. She looked at the front door and thought, *What's to stop me from walking out? What is he going to do, come out onto the street and shoot me?* Ebony stood up and walked toward the door.

"Didn't I tell you not to move?" Ebony heard Nuquan ask, just as she was about to turn the knob. She turned around and was about to respond when his mother walked over to her and took her by the arm.

"Come on, Denise," she said. "This food is ready."

They walked into the kitchen and Ebony pulled out a chair and sat down.

"You like conch, Denise?" Miss Cat asked.

At first Ebony didn't respond.

"Denise?"

"I'm sorry," Ebony said quickly, realizing that Miss Cat was speaking to her.

"I asked if you liked conch. Don't matter, though, 'cause that's all I cooked and I ain't cooking nothing else."

"Yes, ma'am, I like it." Ebony smiled at Miss Cat.

"Well, help yourself. Ain't no maid service around here."

Ebony smiled again and fixed a plate of fried conch, plantains, and coleslaw. She said a quick prayer and dug in. Ebony realized she was starving and ate like a prisoner who'd had her first home-cooked meal after being released, because that's precisely what she was.

"Is it good?" Nuquan's mother asked, looking at Ebony as if she were a rabid animal who'd wandered into her home.

"Yes, ma'am," Ebony mumbled, her mouth full of food. She grabbed a glass of ice water and took a gulp. "Sorry I'm so greedy. Normally I display more home training, but I didn't have breakfast this morning."

Nuquan's mother just nodded and looked at the small television set on the kitchen counter while Ebony refocused her attention on her plate. She continued wolfing down her food.

"That's a damn shame," Ebony heard Nuquan's mother say. "Don't make no sense that all them folks got hurt in that fire."

"Whatever," Nuquan said nonchalantly. "I don't know why you're even wasting your time watching this mess."

"It ain't mess, it's the news. Maybe you should watch it and you'd know a little something about the world."

"I know plenty about the world."

"You can always know more. Ain't nothing wrong with learning something new. You might see something that can help you make some money," Miss Cat said.

"I do all right."

"Did you hear about that fire, Denise?" Miss Cat asked.

"Yes, ma'am. I heard a little something."

"Mm-mm-mm. I don't know what the world is coming to," Miss Cat said, shaking her head. "The reporter said if the building's sprinklers and fire alarms were working, that whole tragedy could have been avoided. Folks got all burnt up and had smoke inhalation. It was just a big mess. One of the girls that died was a black girl. A real pretty one, too."

"Mama, don't nobody care 'bout no damn psychos," Nuquan said.

"Sure they do, don't they, Ebony?" Nuquan's mother asked.

"Yeah," Ebony answered out of habit. Nuquan and Miss Cat stared at her. Ebony dropped her fork. "Fuck," she muttered. She was busted.

CHAPTER SEVEN

Miami Beach

O fficer, I swear I'm innocent," a nearly nude man told Miami Beach Police Violent Crimes detective Marley Parnell.

"Tell it to the judge," she replied. "I'm going to have to take you down to the station."

"Isn't there something I can do, some kind of arrangement we can make?" The man winked at Marley.

"Are you attempting to bribe an officer?" She put the man's arms behind his back and handcuffed him.

"I'm just saying that I'm willing to do anything, and I do mean *anything,* to make this disappear."

"The way you made your clothes disappear?"

"C'mon, Officer. You've got to admit that you like what you see."

Marley stood back and inspected the man's body. "I'll admit, you have a very nice body."

"And I know just what to do with it. I also know just what to do with a body like yours. You may try to cover it up with that uniform, but I can see what's going on underneath."

"Oh, you can, can you? Well, put your money where your mouth is," Marley said, challenging him.

"If you just take the cuffs off, I'll do whatever!"

"I'm not taking the cuffs off. You're just going to have to do what you gotta do without the use of your hands."

Marley stood back and unbuttoned her uniform top, revealing full, perky breasts with hardened nipples.

"Officer, you don't have a bra on."

"And I don't have any panties on either."

Marley stepped out of her uniform pants, showing the man that she was telling the truth. There she stood naked save for the holster that held her service weapon, pepper spray, and nightstick.

"What are you going to do to me?" the man asked, his eyes wide with fear.

"Anything I want to. You're my prisoner now."

Marley pushed the man roughly onto his back, then stood over him, legs spread. She lowered her body slowly until her bald pussy was just inches above his mouth.

"Lick it!" she commanded.

The man stuck his tongue out but couldn't reach her clitoris.

"Come on, you're going to have to do better than that," she teased.

The man continued to lap at her pussy, and every time he got within reach, she'd pull away until he was begging to taste her.

"Please! Please let me lick your pussy," he whimpered.

When Marley was satisfied that he'd begged enough,

she lowered herself onto him, nearly smothering him with her box. The man mumbled beneath her.

"What's that you say? You can't breathe? I don't need you to breathe, I need you to eat." Marley threw her head back and laughed as she allowed the man breathing room. He greedily devoured her dripping snatch, working her clitoris before plunging his long tongue into her canal. Marley rode his face, working her hips at different speeds and angles to maximize her pleasure.

"That's right! Lick this pussy! Oh, shit, I'm about to come!"

Marley clamped the man's head between her thighs like a vise and shouted as she climaxed, her juices running down the side of the man's face.

"I'm not done with you yet!" she said. "You're the one who was displaying the lewd and lascivious behavior, so show me just how lewd and lascivious you can get."

"What do you want me to do?"

"Fuck me good and hard."

"But my hands."

"I'm not trying to fuck your hands. Now let's see what you're working with." Marley climbed off his face and gave the man's underwear a rough tug. "Hmm, I see you've been carrying a concealed weapon. Looks like I'm going to have to disarm you."

Marley hopped on the man's cock and began to rock back and forth, stimulating her G-spot.

"You better do what I said and fuck me good and hard or it's going to be jail time for you," Marley threatened.

The man beneath her began pumping furiously, wincing from the pain of his arms pinned uncomfortably behind him.

"That's right, fuck me!" Marley shouted as she began to come a second time.

"Oh, please, can I come?"

"You know the drill. Beg for it," Marley ordered.

"Please let me come. I don't think I can hold it anymore."

"Okay, wimp, go ahead and bust your nuts."

The man moaned as he released. Marley collapsed on top of him. They lay there for a moment, panting like dogs and trying to catch their breath.

"God, Marley, that was so fucking good."

"Yes it was, Matt," Marley said to her husband of three years. Role-playing had become a regular part of their lovemaking, and since it had, they'd been practically unable to keep their hands off each other.

"Think you can take the cuffs off now?" Matt asked with a laugh. "I need my hands. My editor would be out for your blood if I wasn't able to type anymore."

"Sure, babe." Marley unlocked the cuffs and put them back on her holster. "Your bestsellers pay these bills."

"It's a good thing I don't have to go to a nine-to-five job. If people could see all the sex bruises you've been leaving on me, I'd never live it down." Matt rubbed his wrists, then exclaimed, "Oh, shit!"

"What?" Marley asked, reaching for her pistol and looking around.

"Calm down. Your girl Ebony Knight is on TV, that's all." Matt pointed at the television. "You know, I've been thinking of sending her a thank-you card. Ever since you worked her case, my sex life hasn't been the same!"

"Turn it up," Marley said, watching intently as the news covered the Everglades hospital fire. "That's an interesting turn of events." Marley arched an eyebrow. "Convenient, too."

Marley and her partner were the detectives called to the scene the night of Erik Johansen's and Jeff Cardoza's murders. Since then she'd been unable to erase from her mind the sight of Ebony Knight shaking and covered in blood. She was the most traumatized witness Marley had seen in her four years on the police force. She'd dealt with people who were shaken up, even in shock, but never so disoriented that they had to be transported to a mental hospital.

Afterward she and her partner interviewed Ebony Knight and worked extensively with the crime scene investigators to find out what really happened. Marley had never been satisfied with the conclusions that were drawn. Her gut told her that things were far more complicated than a case of obsession that ended in murder and that Ebony never killed Erik in self-defense. No, something else had happened that evening. Ebony was covering something up, and it never sat right with

Marley that she'd been unable to figure out just what it was.

Marley now had that same feeling in her gut, that woman's intuition tugging at her, telling her that things weren't the way that they appeared to be. Her cell phone rang.

"Parnell," she answered.

"Marley, you're gonna hate me, but you can forget about your day off today. The captain called us in." It was her partner, Emilio "Rocky" Rosa.

"Great," Marley deadpanned. "What's going on?"

"Double homicide and a missing person. Doctor's office in Mid Beach. And I'm warning you, I hear it ain't pretty."

"It never is. Meet you there in fifteen minutes."

Marley got dressed in a hurry and was headed for the door when she decided to reach out to an old friend.

"Kevin, how are you? This is Marley," she said to a friend who worked with the fire department.

"Marley. Long time no hear from. Let me guess. You're divorcing that geek you married and you're ready to run off with me."

"Not this time."

"One of these days, Marley. You'll realize you made a big mistake choosing that lame writer over me."

"And one of these days you're going to realize that you made the choice for me. You were the one who wasn't ready for a commitment, player," Marley teased.

"I was a fool."

"You still are," Marley said, laughing.

"What can I do for you?"

"There was a fire over at the psychiatric hospital in the Glades. I need info."

"Ah, yes, I heard about it. The preliminary report isn't back yet, but you'll be the first person I call when it is."

"Thanks, Kevin. You're the best."

This time, I'm going to get to the bottom of this, Marley swore silently.

Marley walked behind the yellow police tape outside the Miami Beach office building that housed the offices of Dr. Noelle Nesbitt. The first thing that she noticed when she stepped inside was the blood. It was everywhere, as if someone had made it a point to smear it on the walls and track it all over the floor.

"What happened here?" Marley asked a uniformed officer at the crime scene. Her partner, Rocky, joined them and handed Marley a cup of coffee.

"No sign of forced entry. The perp walked in, started shooting, and took out the receptionist. One shot to the chest, two to the forehead, one to the shoulder. Three shots hit the wall." The officer pointed at a blood-splattered wall. A woman's lifeless body was sprawled at an awkward angle, gaping scarlet holes peppering her white cotton shirt.

"We think the person that was sitting here in the waiting area tried to make a run for it. The shooter fired another storm of bullets. There are two points of entry in this victim. One hit the right thigh, the other the left temple at close range." The cop lifted the sheet that was covering a dead body on the floor. The entire left side of the victim's face was missing. Marley flinched and looked away.

"Also, the doctor is missing," the cop said as he walked the detectives through the maze of plastic numbers that tracked shell casings on the floor. "Right now we've got someone looking at the surveillance-camera footage for the building and the elevators. We'll let you know what turns up. Also, the shooter tried to cover his or her tracks. They set fire to the garbage can and a stack of magazines, but the sprinklers put it out before it could amount to anything serious. CSI is seeing if they can lift any prints."

"Thanks," Marley said. "In the meantime, can we get someone from Computer Crimes in to get the patient records from their system? I'll call the DA and make sure that we have a subpoena."

The officer nodded and walked away.

Marley turned to her partner. "My guess is that these homicides were personal."

"Yeah, chances are the doctor knew the perp. Probably a head case with an ax to grind," Rocky said.

"No telling." Marley took a gulp of coffee. "All I can say is that there must be something in the water today. I saw on the news that Everglades Psychiatric Hospital burned down. Your favorite person, Ebony Knight, is presumed dead."

"Is that right?"

"Yep. Her, the roommate, and a security guard all un-accounted for."

"Oh, that sounds suspect," Rocky said.

"Yes, it does."

"I always said that woman was guilty as sin."

"And I always said you were wrong."

"Even now? You're nuts, Marley. I know you can see what's going on here. The fire is a cover-up. Ebony and her roommate set it in order to escape."

"I'll admit that was my first thought, too, but now I don't know. That just doesn't sound like Ebony Knight's style, plus the fire did break out at a mental hospital. There's so many scenarios as to what could have hap-pened. For all we know, Ebony's roommate could have had some kind of episode, set the fire, kidnapped her and the security guard, and is holding them hostage some-where."

"I bet it's the other way around. That woman would have done anything to get out of the hospital. Ebony always said she didn't belong in Everglades and I agree. She belonged on death row!" Rocky's voice was filled with disgust.

"What did you have against Ebony Knight?"

"You mean other than the fact that she was a mur-derer?"

"A court of law said she killed in self-defense," Marley said, correcting him.

"Whatever," Rocky said with a wave of his hand,

frowning. "She was a freak. She's a part of what's wrong with society."

"Not hardly. The men that went to her are the freaks. If it weren't for them, she wouldn't have even had a business. Plus, she ran that business within the confines of the law."

"So she said."

"So the evidence says. We checked her out thoroughly, and all we could find out was that she ran a legal operation. I think that a chauvinist pig like you was just pissed that she was making so much cake off stupid rich guys who had a hard-on for being treated like shit." Marley laughed.

"Oink, oink," Rocky snorted. "Call me a pig all you want, but women belong barefoot and in the kitchen and either knocked up or taking care of kids. They have no business taking money for kinky acts, and they certainly don't belong on the police force. They should leave that for the men." Rocky winked at Marley.

"Funny," she said sarcastically.

"Anyway, what's with you siding with a perp?"

"What are you talking about?"

"You seemed to really take a liking to Mistress Ebony Knight. You were fascinated by her. If I didn't know better, I'd say you were a closet freak yourself."

"You gotta admit she was intriguing. Twenty-five years old and a millionaire all from selling a kinky fantasy with no sex. And she was connected to one of the most powerful men in the state, possibly even the country. Besides, I didn't take a liking or a disliking to her. I was there to gather the facts in a nonbiased fashion, and the evidence didn't add up to me."

"Cops can't always go with the evidence. Sometimes you've gotta go with your gut. She played crazy to get away with murder and collect a fat check. You're too blinded by your girl-crush on her to see what's right in front of your face. See, the thing about chicks like you and this Ebony Knight here is that you think you can do anything that a man can do. You walk around like you've got big hairy ones between your legs . . ."

Detective Parnell half listened to her partner as he continued to spew his know-it-all knowledge of women at her. Rocky was a good cop, but sometimes he got on her nerves with his sexist ways of thinking.

"Detectives, I think we have something." The uniformed police officer who'd spoken to them earlier returned. "Another fire. Definitely connected."

"Where?" Rocky asked.

"Dr. Nesbitt's home. She lives over on La Gorce Island."

"Let's go," Marley said.

"We've got serious spatter," the crime scene investigator told Marley and Rocky when they arrived at a gorgeous million-dollar home. "We're running the blood right now. There's a pool in the kitchen and a trail leading from the house to the driveway."

"Let me guess. Dr. Nesbitt's car is missing?" Marley asked.

"Yeah. And this old Thunderbird was left in its place."

"Any prints?"

"A couple smudged ones. Looks like someone tried to set the vehicle on fire, but it stopped burning. There's spilled accelerant leading to the house, but no signs of attempted ignition. Whoever did this was in a hurry."

"Someone was very unhappy with their therapy," Rocky said.

"Obviously. Have the patient lists been accessed yet?" Marley asked the crime scene investigator.

"Yes."

Rocky's cell phone rang and he stepped aside to answer the call.

"Good. Run the prints from the car through AFIS, see if any hits come up for arsonists and if any of the names match our patient list. I'm pretty sure this isn't our perp's first time at the rodeo. Any prints found at the primary scene?" Marley asked.

"No, not yet. But if we find any, we'll cross-check them."

"You're not going to believe this, but we've got another fire," Rocky told Marley.

"We don't work for the fire department. What the fuck is going on here?" Marley asked, irritated. "Where's this fire?"

"This time it isn't a where as much as it's a who."

"Huh?"

"We don't have to look for Dr. Nesbitt anymore. She was found in front of a synagogue on Alton Road. Someone doused her with gasoline and set her on fire. She's dead."

"Something tells me this is gonna be a long day," Marley said.

CHAPTER EIGHT

Carol City

I told you, Nu-Nu! I told you it was her! I never forget a face, and hers has been plastered all over the news!" Miss Cat screamed excitedly.

"Well, I'll be damned," Nuquan said. "You were right."

"I thought you was supposed to be dead. They said you died in that hospital fire. I just saw the story right before y'all got here. Ooh, Nu-Nu, I bet you there's a reward if we turn her in!" Miss Cat looked at Ebony and licked her chops like a jackal about to devour its prey.

"There's no reward," Ebony said.

"How you know?" Nuquan asked.

"I didn't escape from jail, it was a mental hospital. And I wasn't supposed to be there in the first place."

"Yeah, right," Nuquan said. "Let's call the police and see what they're offering for her."

"Did you forget you were involved in a shoot-out and that there's a stolen truck in your garage?" Ebony asked. "Sure, go ahead and call the police."

"Nuquan, don't listen to her. She the crazy person. You think the police are gonna believe her? You can pin all that shit that went down on her. She stole that truck. You can say she was the one shooting outside the store and then she took you hostage."

"Please," Ebony said with a wave of her hand. "Something tells me that this one definitely has a criminal record. He don't want the police nowhere near here." Ebony pointed a slender finger at Nuquan.

"I wonder what's wrong with her?" Miss Cat asked Nuquan as if Ebony weren't sitting there.

"There's nothing wrong with me!"

"Then why were you locked up?" Nuquan asked.

"It's a long story, but to make it short, I was set up."

"Yeah, she's crazy all right. Crazy people always talking about they been framed for something." Miss Cat laughed.

"I'm not crazy!" Ebony shouted.

"Didn't you burn the hospital down?" Nuquan asked. "That's crazy."

"Look, it isn't what you think."

"People got hurt, you know," Miss Cat said.

"I didn't mean for that to happen, but I had something to take care of that couldn't wait."

"What?" Miss Cat asked. "Look to me like you been chillin'. You got on new clothes, and I know it because that don't look like no hospital gear. Plus you got some more in the bags in my living room. And you been hanging out with my son. You break out just to do that?"

"I wouldn't call what your son and I were doing hanging out. He carjacked me!"

Miss Cat waved Ebony's accusation aside and instead looked at her as if she were on display at a museum.

"So what they said on the news is true? Were you a domi-dominati—" Miss Cat struggled with the pronunciation of the word.

"I was a dominatrix, yes."

"And you killed that billionaire dude?" Nuquan asked.

"No, *that's* not true."

"That's what the news said. Said you killed him and got off on self-defense because he was stalking you. I remember that story because once I saw that your little skinny self pulled a billionaire, I was thinking about trying to be one of them domination girls, too! They ain't ready for this jelly though!" Miss Cat cackled.

"You don't want no parts of what I was caught up in, trust me. That man stalked me and made my life miserable."

"Some folks would love to have your misery. I remember them saying you ran a multimillion-dollar business and you lived in that fat-ass crib on the ocean."

"All that glitters isn't gold," Ebony told Miss Cat.

"Fuck that. Nu-Nu, gimme Ms. Thing's purse over there."

"Excuse me! I don't think so!" Ebony clutched her purse. Nuquan pulled it roughly off her arm and handed it to his mother. Miss Cat's eyes widened as she peered inside Ebony's bag. She dumped the contents of the purse onto the table.

"Damn!" Nuquan said. "Looka here, looka here now."

Miss Cat grabbed a handful of Ebony's money and began to count it.

"I need to ask you something. And you better think long and hard before you answer," Nuquan said to Ebony.

"Whatever."

"Twice today you've said you've got something important to do. Well, we can let you go do it, but first we need to know how much is your freedom worth to you?"

"What?"

"Are you willing to part with this cash in order for us to let you go?" Miss Cat got straight to the point.

"So you *are* kidnapping me? You want my money as ransom or something? Fine. Take it. Just let me walk."

"Oh, hell no!" Miss Cat exclaimed. "That was a test and you just failed."

"You gotta be fucking kidding me."

"Nope. I estimate you got about fifteen or twenty thousand dollars here," Miss Cat said, shuffling bills through her fingertips. "If you're willing to walk away from this so easily, there must be a whole lot more where that came from."

"Look, I don't even know how much money I have. I'm not in control of my finances anymore. You could very well be taking everything I have left to my name. Isn't that good enough for you?"

"Nope," Nuquan said.

"The way I see it, you need to find out what you got left to your name. And you need to go on and tell us what's so important that you've got to do."

"I think she's gonna get her hands on some more of her money. That's what I think. Otherwise she would be pitching a bitch about this cash," Nuquan told his mom.

"I think you're right, Son."

"The both of you are wrong," Ebony said, shaking her head.

"Then why don't you set us straight," Miss Cat replied.

Ebony folded her arms and didn't say anything.

"Have it your way, but you're not going anywhere until you talk," Nuquan told her.

"Says who?"

"Says me." Nuquan then pointed to the gun in his waistband. "And him."

An hour later Ebony was still sitting at the kitchen table with Nuquan and his mother. She'd filled the time with daydreams. Some were of happier moments, like her college graduation and how proud her mother had been, and the day that Jeff proposed. Some of her daydreams were reflections on times filled with drama and anguish, like how she felt when Jeff broke up with her, how devastated she was as she watched him killed right in front of her, and how obliterated she was when Dr. St.

John told her that her mother was dead. This cocktail of diverse memories fueled her purpose. There was no way that she was going to let the deaths of the two people that meant the most to her go unavenged. Right or wrong she was going to kill Carmelita Sanchez in their honor, despite the obstacles that stood in her way.

Ebony was growing impatient but didn't let on. She was simply waiting for the perfect opportunity to make her escape. She had to get out of these crazy people's house and continue on her mission. The more time that elapsed, the more difficult getting her revenge could become. Eventually the arson investigators would discover that her body was not in the building. The police would figure out the security guard's truck was missing, and then it would only be a matter of time before people started looking for her. It was time for action.

Ebony moaned, clutching her midsection.

"What's wrong with you?" Miss Cat asked.

"My stomach."

"What you trying to say? You ain't like my food? What, my food making you sick now?"

"No, it's not that." Ebony peered into the waistband of her pants. "It's cramps. I can't believe this shit. I have the worst luck. First I get caught up in this mess, and now my cycle just started early." Ebony groaned. "Can I use your bathroom?"

"That's nasty," Nuquan said.

His mother rolled her eyes at him. "It's the second door on the left," Miss Cat said, pointing down the hall.

"You think I could take a shower? I feel a little not-so-fresh, if you know what I mean."

"It's clean towels in the cabinet under the sink. It's pads in there, too," Miss Cat said absentmindedly, thumbing through a stack of bills, then fanning herself with the money.

From the living room, Ebony got the bag of clothes she'd bought earlier and went into the bathroom, locking the door behind her. She turned the water on in the tub, then looked at the window. She smiled. There wasn't a pane-glass window and she was glad, because it would probably have had bars on the outside of it. What she saw was even better: a jalousie window.

Ebony stood near the door and listened for motion. She didn't hear any, but she knew that she didn't have much time. She turned on the shower. Then she cranked open the jalousie and used a shaving knife she found in the medicine cabinet to loosen the screws that held the glass panels in their slots, then placed the panels on the bathroom rug. When she'd removed half of them, she saw that she had enough room to fit through the window. She hopped out of it and into the backyard. Ebony didn't get two steps before she heard a dreaded sound: the low growl of a dog behind her.

Ebony froze. She hated dogs. And worse than that, dogs hated her. She prayed the dog wouldn't bark and alert Miss Cat and Nuquan, and she prayed even harder that it wouldn't bite. Then she ran. She didn't look back, she didn't hesitate, she just hit the chain-link fence in front of her and climbed as fast as she could. But it wasn't fast enough. She felt herself being pulled with great force from the fence. Ebony muttered a one-word prayer—"Jesus"—as she felt her body crash to the ground.

CHAPTER NINE

Downtown Miami

People lined up against the wall of the building that housed the federal prison. Despite the ninety-degree temperature everyone was dressed in unseasonably warm clothes because of the dress code, adding to the frustration and irritation that usually accompanies visiting a loved one in the pretrial detention center. The line inched along at a snail's pace, children growing restless and babies getting fussy. Some people had been in the line for over an hour, and the end of the two-hour visiting period was creeping closer.

"I swear these corrections officers seem to take a perverse pleasure in making this experience as slow and miserable as possible," a woman wearing a modestly cut, light blue pants suit complained to the man in line next to her.

"They sure do. And they don't have any manners. They treat us so rudely. There's no reason for the attitude. We didn't do anything, and as far as they know, the people we're visiting didn't do anything either. But, oh no! They think everyone here is a lowlife. So much for innocent until proven guilty," he commiserated, wiping his brow with a handkerchief.

The street beside the building was empty. Cars hadn't been allowed to access the road since 9/11, and it was barricaded on both ends, but that didn't stop a late-model Volvo from crashing through the wooden horses with Do Not Enter written on their sides. The car left a set of skid marks on the concrete as it jerked to an awkward stop and the driver got out.

"Oh, shit!" the woman in the blue suit yelled, pointing at the car.

"Everyone down!" a corrections officer screamed as the driver pulled out a gun and waved it in the air.

The line of visitors did the exact opposite, scattering like jacks on the sidewalk. The gunman shot into the sky, yelling something incoherent before running across the street. Suddenly the car burst into flames. Seconds later it exploded.

Police cars and fire trucks surrounded the car, which had been reduced to nothing more than a heap of burnt metal and plastic. Finding fingerprints would be impossible. Two uniformed police officers interviewed the few people who lingered at the scene, but the only information that they could glean was that the person who'd set the car on fire was a short, thin female with long, dark hair.

One of the officers spied an electronics store across

the street from where the explosion had taken place. Televisions and video cameras filled the display window, and surveillance cameras were mounted around the store's façade.

"Check it out," he said to his partner, pointing at the store.

"Let's see if Big Brother is really always watching," his partner replied.

The officers flashed their badges at the man behind the counter, and within minutes with the assistance of the store's owner they were in a back room watching the tapes recorded from several different cameras' vantage points.

"There!" one of the officers said. "Freeze it right there. We need a printout of that frame."

"Terrorist?" the officer's partner asked.

"I don't know. But we'd better make sure that the feds, Homeland Security, and local law enforcement all get a copy of this."

Miami Beach, Noon

"Today has to be one of the most morbid days I've had since I made detective, and it's only noon," Marley said to her partner. They'd just left the Miami Beach synagogue where Dr. Noelle Nesbitt's body had been found. The smell of burned flesh lingered in Marley's nostrils and made her feel queasy, but Rocky was busy munching on an arepa he'd picked up from a sidewalk vendor.

"I don't see how you can eat after what we've seen today," she said as they got into their unmarked Crown Victoria. Marley had been on the police force for four years, two of them as a Violent Crimes detective, but she never became desensitized to the sight of dead bodies the way some of her colleagues had. Every time she saw one, no matter what the circumstances surrounding the death, she lost her appetite.

"I hunger, therefore I eat," Rocky said. "This is why I say women shouldn't be cops. Do you need to pull over to puke?" he teased.

"No. And you can make fun of me all you want. I don't care what you say, you've got to be inhuman to not feel at least a little nauseous when you see what we just saw. Come on, admit it. That was some twisted shit."

"Okay, I'll admit it. What kind of person sets a woman on fire while she's still alive and lets her burn to death?"

"A real sicko." Marley frowned. "I still can't believe that we haven't been able to get a good ID on this perp. How do you not notice somebody setting another person on fire in front of a synagogue in Miami Beach? Seriously, how does some nosy blue hair not see something at the least? They seem to see every damn thing else."

"Ah, just another day in paradise." Rocky finished off his arepa. "See no evil, hear no evil, speak no evil, unless the evil is happening to you."

Marley's cell phone rang.

"Marley, it's Kevin. I just wanted to let you know that the preliminary report came back on the Everglades fire."

"Awesome. What can you tell me?"

"Definitely arson. There were accelerants used, multiple points of origin, a couple different flash points, and from what I can see a couple explosions. The fire started in one of the rooms and spread down the hallway and into the kitchen, where it grew more."

"What about bodies?"

"There were three expected, but only one found. The security guard."

"I'll be damned. Thanks a bunch, Kev. I owe you one," Marley said, disconnecting the call.

"What was that about?" Rocky asked.

"That was my connection at the fire department. I called him when I saw the story about Everglades."

"I knew you had a crush on that dominatrix."

"Get over it already, Rocky. I had a hunch, same as you. But unlike you, I scratched below the surface, and it's a good thing that I did. My source said that there was only one body found in the rubble. The security guard."

"So my theory is right. Those crazy broads escaped from the hospital. And they killed the security guard in order to do it."

"I don't know about all that, but there's only one way to truly find out." Marley grinned at Rocky.

"I don't like that look. What are you up to?"

"Nothing. I'm just thinking I got my appetite back,"

Marley said. "Feel like grabbing a little lunch? I know you just ate an arepa, but I'm sure you'll find somewhere to put a little more food." Marley poked Rocky's flabby midsection with her finger.

"Very funny. Where did you have in mind?"

"Just sit back and enjoy the ride."

"Have you seen this woman?"

Marley and Rocky had posed the question dozens of times to every business owner in the area surrounding where Everglades Psychiatric Hospital once stood. The inquiry was accompanied by two photographs, both torn from a newspaper article on the fire. One was of Ebony Knight and the other of Kira Long. No one had seen either until Marley and Rocky reached a truck stop nestled into a deserted area about five miles east of the hospital.

"I saw her earlier this morning," the clerk told Marley, pointing at the picture of Ebony.

"Are you sure it was this woman?"

"Fairly sure. I mean, all you colored gals kind of look alike to me, but she looks like the one. We don't get many of you around here."

Marley flinched at the words "colored gals." *Fucking hillbilly.*

"I can't tell you the last time two of you came in here so close together. Must have been a coon's age. No pun intended." The clerk flashed Marley a snarky grin.

Marley wanted to give the clerk a piece of her mind, or better yet, a piece of her foot in her ass. Thankfully Rocky intervened.

"Try and remember exactly when you saw her."

"I don't have to try. It was right after the fire at the funny farm. I remember thinking to myself that the gal what come in here looked like she had ashes in her hair and soot on her face. And she had on the kind of clothes I'd imagine they'd wear there. T-shirt and khaki pants."

"Why didn't you alert the authorities?" Marley asked, irritated.

"Ain't my job. Plus I didn't hear nothing about a reward being offered."

"Can you remember anything else about this woman, aside from the fact that she's colored? Did you see what kind of car she was driving? Do you know what direction she was headed?" Marley asked.

"Can't say that I do. Now is that it? I had to work a double shift and I'm not in the mood for any more questions." The clerk unfolded a *National Enquirer* and began to read.

Marley rolled her eyes. "Rocky, I think we're done here."

"What a bitch," Marley fumed when they were back at the car.

"You're one to talk. You said we were going to get something to eat, but instead we're out here in the hot-ass swamp."

"Sorry, partner. But it was worth it. Now we've got a positive ID on Ebony Knight."

"You and this damned dominatrix," Rocky fussed. "What's the point of all this? Did you forget that we have three homicides from this morning to solve?"

"The point is we're going to figure out once and for all what happened the night that Erik Johansen died. We're going to find Ebony Knight."

"You're never going to get the truth out of that one. The truth isn't in her."

"Doesn't have to be in her," Marley said. "Because I'm going to find it no matter where it is."

Miami Beach, 3:30 p.m.

"Where the hell have the two of you been?" Captain Matthias Webster fumed at Marley and Rocky when they returned to the police station. "I called both of your phones over an hour ago."

"Sorry, Captain. Rocky and I were covering a lead out in the Everglades. The reception is horrible out there. But wait until you hear what we found out," Marley enthused.

"Let me guess. You figured out that Ebony Knight and Kira Long escaped from the hospital."

"How'd you know?" Marley asked, shocked.

"Because we found out the same thing an hour ago.

That's what I was calling to tell the two of you. The arson investigator's office called and informed us that the only body that was found belonged to the security guard. Not only that, but Kira Long was spotted setting fire to a car outside the pretrial detention center downtown."

"No way," Marley said.

"Officers caught her on the surveillance camera from the electronics store across the street. Also, the homicides from this morning were most likely Kira Long's work. Turns out she's a former patient of Dr. Nesbitt's."

Marley smiled at Rosa, who frowned and crossed his arms.

"Well, we've already gotten a positive ID on Knight. A gas station clerk saw her the night of the fire. As far as the clerk knows, Knight was alone. My guess is that the two of them escaped together but went their separate ways," Marley told Captain Webster.

"Contact anyone that either of the ladies might go to for help. They aren't going to be able to get too far on their own. I don't want this to get any farther out of hand than it already has. Before the media jumps in and has a field day, let's get these ladies off the streets and back into custody where they belong."

"So where are we off to first? You're the expert on Ebony Knight, so I'm sure you have a master plan already brewing," Rocky said sarcastically.

"As a matter of fact, I do. I figure we need to start with the doctor from Everglades. She can tell us the kind of mental state the women were in," Marley suggested.

"Think she's going to break doctor-patient privilege in order to help us?"

"She'd better."

I have nothing to say to you," Dr. St. John said when Marley and Rocky turned up on her doorstep and flashed their badges.

She started to close the door, but Marley forced it open.

"Really? Because I think you do," Marley said.

"No. I don't want to talk to you. I'm not in the mood. It's been a horrible day. And you can't come in here without a search warrant."

"We're not interested in searching the premises. We need information about Kira Long and Ebony Knight. We have reason to believe that they started the fire and used it as a cover up to escape," Rocky said.

"An escape? Go on," the doctor said, continuing to stand in the doorway.

"So far, Kira's old doctor, Noelle Nesbitt, is dead. Kira burned her alive this morning. The receptionist at Dr. Nesbitt's office and an innocent patient are also dead. They were shot to death. For all we know there could be other victims. So are we going to have to do this the hard way or the easy way?" Marley stood with her hands on her hips.

"Come in, Detectives," Dr. St. John said, opening the

door. "I apologize if I seemed a little uncooperative, but I've been in a terrible mood ever since I talked to Marisol Rivera-Frye this morning. I want to help you but I don't know how I can."

"You can start by telling us exactly who we're dealing with," Rocky said.

The doctor sighed and nodded. "Ebony Knight is one of the biggest regrets of my career. She should have never been detained in Everglades. Ebony always claimed that she was innocent. Even though Erik Johansen's death was ruled self-defense, she swore that she didn't kill him. She also said that her medical records were forged and that she didn't have any history of mental illness."

"Don't most of your patients make similar claims?" Rocky asked.

"Yes, that's why I recommended her for further psychiatric evaluation. I thought that I had evidence of her illness in black and white, so I went with it instead of listening to her. Ebony even tried to warn me that her mother was in danger, and I didn't listen and now she's dead. I messed up big-time."

"And what about Kira Long?" Rocky asked.

"Kira is another story altogether. She's one of the most disturbed patients that I've ever treated. She's delusional, she lacks impulse control, she feels no sense of remorse, she's a textbook psychopath with many underlying illnesses. Her issues stem mostly from her traumatic childhood. She was adopted when she was a toddler after having been removed from a home that was, let's just say, less than ideal. Any horror you can imagine, Kira went through before she could even walk."

"Are these women dangerous?" Marley asked.

"Kira definitely is. And I'm sorry, but I have no idea where she might strike next. Kira spends most of her time in a fantasy world. It's impossible to apply any logic to her actions. She thinks that everyone is out to get her."

"And Ebony?"

"She only thought one person was out to get her: her conservator, Carmelita Sanchez. Ebony told me in a therapy session that she believed Carmelita was trying to take her life, and in light of recent events I have every reason to believe that she was telling the truth."

"Was Ebony angry enough with Carmelita to try and get revenge?"

"I can't say definitively that Ebony Knight was violent, so I won't go as far as to say that she'd go after revenge. But she was angry, and justifiably so. I do believe that she'd go to desperate measures to clear her name and get her life back. She blamed Carmelita for everything. If you want answers about Ebony Knight, find Carmelita Sanchez. As for Kira, the best move would be to alert the media about her escape and appeal to the community to assist you in locating her. You're not going to find her any other way."

SEX APPEAL

Miami, 5 p.m.

"I bet this Carmelita Sanchez is dirty," Marley said to Rocky with confidence.

"If she is, then she and Ebony were in cahoots and it went wrong. Ebony Knight was no angel," Rocky said.

"We'll see."

Marley parked the navy blue unmarked Crown Victoria she was driving in front of a steel-and-glass monster of a building.

"Ms. Sanchez is definitely gonna be slick from the looks of this building. Only people out to deceive and impress would locate their business in such a pretentious-looking place," Marley observed as they rode to the twenty-third floor in a futuristic-looking elevator.

The receptionist at the front desk of Rios, Stein and Black tried to give Rocky and Marley the runaround when they arrived.

"Ms. Sanchez does not see visitors without an appointment. She's usually in between ten and six. I'll be more than happy to check her schedule for an opening." The woman raked her short, square-shaped, bloodred fingernails over her taut chignon and pursed her lips.

"This is a police matter of extreme importance," Marley informed her. "We could really use her assistance."

"Do you have a warrant?"

"It's nothing that serious," Marley said, glancing sideways at Rocky.

"Ms. Sanchez is in a meeting for the remainder of the day," the receptionist told them curtly as she gave them the once-over. "But I'd be more than happy to leave word with her that you visited."

Something told Marley that this woman had never been more than happy to do anything in her entire life.

"We won't take up much of her time. As I stated, this matter is really of the utmost importance. Ms. Sanchez could be a huge help to the department. We'll remember how cooperative she was when she needs us. Or we'll have to remember how uncooperative she was." Marley gave the receptionist a steely look.

"Let me see what I can do." The receptionist disappeared behind a frosted-glass-and-chrome door.

"Wonder why Sanchez is so reclusive," Marley said. "Her guard dog really has her hackles up."

"Maybe Carmelita really is in a meeting. Let's just see what happens."

The door opened and the receptionist returned with a beautiful woman wearing a white Dolce & Gabbana pantsuit with her hair pulled tightly in a bun like the receptionist's. Marley wondered if that was coincidental.

"Detectives? I'm Carmelita Sanchez."

"I'm Detective Emilio Rosa, and this is my partner, Detective Marley Parnell. We'd like to talk with you for a moment. We know that you're very busy and we promise not to take too long." Rocky stared at Carmelita, practically salivating.

Carmelita smiled warmly as she extended her hand.

Marley noticed an exquisite diamond tennis bracelet with large, clear stones, dangling from her slim wrist. *This woman is definitely doing all right for herself,* she thought. *That bracelet is probably worth my entire year's salary.*

"Let's go into my office, shall we?" Carmelita led the detectives down a long hallway with walls covered in contemporary art and into an office with a breathtaking view of Biscayne Bay and the Atlantic Ocean.

"This is a lovely office, Ms. Sanchez," Marley said. "You must be one hell of an attorney. Maybe I should have gone to law school."

"Thanks, but please, call me Carmelita."

"Well, Carmelita, we're sure that you've heard about the fire at Everglades Psychiatric Hospital. Your conservatee, Ebony Knight, is believed to have perished in that fire," Marley said.

Carmelita shook her head sadly. "Ebony was more than just a client, she was my friend. My very best friend. We met in college and were tighter than sisters ever since. It's all so surreal to me how things turned out. As you can imagine, I'm quite distraught. I'm sure I may look pulled together, but I assure you that it is a front. Inside my heart is breaking," Carmelita said dramatically.

Marley and Rocky exchanged a look.

"Did Ms. Knight's mental state ever cause you alarm before the night of the murders?" Rocky asked.

"Yes, I have to admit that it did. Sometimes she'd act like a totally different person than the Ebony I knew and loved. There was one time that sticks out in my mind from a while back. It was when my mom died and she was supposed to be comforting me. To this day I don't know what set her off, but she punched me and we had a knock-down, drag-out fight. I don't know what got into her. She was like that sometimes, violent and cruel." Carmelita dabbed at her eyes with a tissue. "It was because of her illness, I know. When she wasn't having an episode, she was the sweetest and kindest person you'd ever want to meet. And she was so smart, a borderline genius. I don't know why she settled on being a dominatrix. Ebony could have been anything, a lawyer, a doctor. She could have really made a difference in the world."

"So you disapproved of your friend's profession?" Rocky asked.

"Despite the power suit and executive hairdo, I'm far from a prude, and I'm certainly not a judgmental person. People's personal kink is their own business. But I thought that it was dangerous."

"And why is that?" Marley asked.

"The obvious reasons. I'm sure I don't have to tell you the things that can happen to women in those types of professions."

"Did she ever talk about Erik Johansen?" Rocky asked.

"Well, Erik Johansen from all accounts was a strange bird. I never met him personally, but from what Ebony told me, he was kind of disturbed. I wouldn't have dealt with him at all if I were her, but I can definitely understand why she did. He was very wealthy and very generous. He gave her any and every thing she ever wanted."

"Carmelita, I need to ask you this question and please don't take offense, but do you think that Ebony really killed Erik Johansen in self-defense?" Rocky asked.

"I absolutely did when I defended her, but now sometimes I can't help but wonder. But what criminal attorney doesn't have doubts with their clients? It's a part of the territory. An attorney's job is to make sure their client has the best defense possible, regardless of innocence or guilt."

"Had Ms. Knight ever talked about escaping Everglades?" Marley asked.

"She wanted out of course. Who wouldn't? But, no, she never talked about escaping. I thought Ebony was dead. Did she escape?" Carmelita asked wide-eyed.

"No. We just think that the fire may have been started during a botched escape attempt," Rocky said.

Carmelita looked from Rocky to Marley. "Why aren't the fire department's investigators asking me these questions?"

"It really isn't their jurisdiction," Marley explained. "They just determine *how* the fire started, not *why*."

"Yes, well, I suppose that does make sense. Oh. Well, I really must be getting back to my meeting." Carmelita glanced at her wristwatch. "But if you need anything else, please don't hesitate to call me." Carmelita extracted two business cards from an eelskin case and handed them to Rocky and Marley.

"Fancy," Marley said sarcastically, holding up the card before pocketing it as she and Rocky exited the office.

"So what do you think?" Rocky asked.

"I think that she's definitely hiding something beneath all that drama."

"And I hate to say it, but I think that you're right. She definitely doesn't know that Ebony escaped. "

"So do you think Carmelita Sanchez set Ebony up?"

"I'm not going to go that far. I think that there was so much money involved that they turned against each other."

"I'm telling you, you're wrong. We just met our murderer. I just know it," Marley said.

Rocky and Marley got in their unmarked squad car. Soon after, Carmelita exited the building and walked quickly to a parking garage. She was so engrossed in her thoughts that she didn't notice the navy Crown Victoria trailing her.

"Wonder where she's going?" Marley asked.

"Don't lose her and we'll find out," Rocky replied.

Moments later they were on the trail of a silver convertible Mercedes SLR McLaren.

"Run the plate. Let's get Ms. Sanchez's address just in case," Marley said.

Rocky read the license plate numbers over the radio to the dispatcher. Within minutes dispatch had an ID on the tag.

"Go ahead, Dispatch," Rocky said into the car's radio.

"The car is registered to Ebony Knight, 19436 Collins Ave. in Sunny Isles," the dispatcher said over a staticky connection.

"Well, well, well," Marley said, turning to Rocky and smiling. "That's interesting."

"It doesn't mean anything. Keep your eyes on the road," Rocky grumbled.

CHAPTER TEN

Ebony closed her eyes and lay on the grass in a tense ball as she waited to feel canine teeth tearing into her skin and mauling her into a million pieces, but it never came.

"Get up!" a masculine voice boomed.

Ebony opened her eyes. The sun was shining in her face, but when she squinted, she could make out a tall man—at least six feet four—with rippling muscles bulging from beneath a black wifebeater, standing above her holding a vicious-looking pit bull on a leash.

"Who the hell are you and why are you climbing out my mom's window?" the man asked.

Ebony was afraid but couldn't help noticing how fine the man was. His scowl only seemed to enhance his piercing eyes and chiseled jaw, which was covered with a glossy, well-groomed beard. His body was pure perfection— lean, athletic, and hard—and he looked like he put in work in the bedroom. She was so taken aback that she could barely come up with an excuse. Ebony stammered as she struggled to come up with an answer. She was so close to freedom, and she knew saying the wrong thing would land her right back where she started, inside the house with Nuquan and Miss Cat.

"I said, get up!" the man commanded. The dog beside him snarled and looked ready to pounce.

"I think I might be lost," Ebony said, eyeing the dog.

"You're lucky I got him on this leash. But I can always let him go. Start talking."

"Why don't you ask your mom and brother why I'm climbing out of their window? They're the ones who've kidnapped me and have been holding me hostage," Ebony said, rising from the ground and dusting herself off.

"Go back in the house," the man commanded, pointing at the back door.

Fuck it, Ebony thought. *I can go back in the house with these fools. It's better than being eaten by a dog, and if I escaped Everglades, I can damn sure escape this house. I just need to perfect a plan.*

She did as she was told and the man followed her, leaving the dog to run free in the yard.

"Come on," he said as he took Ebony by the arm and led her back into the house. Ebony tingled at the man's touch. *Damn, I'm tweaking! This is not the time for me to be horny. But it's been a long time since I had any and I'm only human. This dude looks so fucking good.* Then she felt guilty, as if she were cheating on Jeff. She admonished herself. *Stay focused!*

"Mama, what's going on?" the man asked. "I just came

in through the back and I caught this woman climbing out the bathroom window."

"Ain't this about a bitch?" Miss Cat said as she saw Ebony enter the house with her other son. "You tried to pull a fast one."

"She says you and Nuquan kidnapped her and are holding her hostage. Please tell me that's not true. You know that's not how we operate."

"She didn't get kidnapped, she was just in the wrong place at the wrong time. Your brother had a little incident this morning. He ran into some Jamaicans that don't want him operating in their territory, and they tried to blast him. He took her truck in order to get away. She just happened to still be inside of it."

"So he carjacked her?"

"I wouldn't go saying all that. It's not like he planned on doing it. What was your brother supposed to do, stand there and get shot? Like I said, she was just in the wrong place at the wrong time. He did what he had to do in order to get away."

"So why haven't you let her go yet? Is she planning on going to the police?"

"Boy, ain't you seen the news today? This lady here busted out that mental hospital in the Everglades. Set the place on fire. She can't go to the police."

"Well, what do you need with her?"

"She's loaded. If the hospital or the police aren't offering a reward for her, she got more than enough money to break us off to keep our mouths shut about seeing her."

"So you're crazy?" the man asked Ebony.

"No, I'm not crazy. Listen, um, what's your name?"

"Fuquan, but you can call me Monk. Everybody does."

Ebony couldn't contain her laughter. "Are you fucking serious? No offense, Miss Cat, but what the fuck were you thinking when you named your children Nuquan and Fuquan?"

"Their daddy named them," Miss Cat replied, unfazed by Ebony's mockery.

"Whatever," Ebony said, pulling herself together. "Listen, Monk, it's a very long story, but in short I was set up. I was never supposed to be in that place and I busted out the hospital to set things straight."

"So you want to clear your name?" Monk asked.

"Yes, something like that."

"What did they think was wrong with you?"

"Everything," Ebony said.

"Remember that rich dude that got himself killed in that fancy crib on the beach?" Miss Cat asked her son.

"Nope. I don't keep up with shit like that."

"It don't matter. This is the woman who killed him after he stalked her and shot her boyfriend. And she got his insurance money. Three million dollars."

"Word?" the man asked.

"That's not exactly the way it all went down. I didn't kill anyone. See, the woman I thought was my lawyer and my best friend did all the killing."

"Why she do that?" Miss Cat asked.

"I don't know. Jealousy. Evil. Greed. Take your pick. When I got locked up, she got herself appointed as my conservator. She's in control of all my assets."

"You must be richer than a motherfucker for someone to go through all that trouble to get they hands on your money," Miss Cat suggested, her eyebrow raised.

"Something like that," Ebony said nonchalantly. "At least, I was at one time."

"I knew you had money," Nuquan said.

"How much money you talking about?" Monk asked.

"A lot. But like I said, I don't even know how much of it is left. That's why I've got to get to that bitch Carmelita. I want my money and then I want revenge."

Nuquan, Miss Cat, and Monk held a silent conversation with their eyes.

"How bad you want to get your money back?" Miss Cat eventually asked.

"Y'all don't really need to be worried about all that."

"The way I see it, I think we do. See, you're not leaving this house alive unless we get our cut," Nuquan said.

"Of what?" Ebony gave him an incredulous look.

"Of your money," Miss Cat said.

"Why would I cut you in on my money?" Ebony asked.

"Because we can make you or break you. We can make sure that things go smoothly for you. Look at you. You riding around in a stolen truck, a stolen *red* truck, trying to be incognito. You getting caught in cross fire in the hood and your face is on TV every fifteen minutes.

If I recognized you, someone else will, too. You talking about clearing your name, but the way you're doing it is bogus as hell," Miss Cat said.

"And you could do a better job?" Ebony asked.

"Hell, yeah. We the tightest crime family in Miami," Nuquan said. "We can keep you under the radar until you don't need to be anymore."

"We're not a crime family," Monk said. "But we can help you lie low."

"All you want to help is yourself to my money. You must think I'm stupid or something. If you were so tight, you wouldn't have been shot at this morning, and you damn sure wouldn't have been walking around the hood," Ebony snapped. "You'd have been in your own whip."

"My car is at my girl's house. I just ran around the corner to get a blunt so we could blaze. Don't get it twisted. We put in work," Nuquan said.

"Yeah, you're putting in so much work you live in Carol City. Looks like you're poor pimping to me," Ebony said, rolling her eyes.

"We may not live in a fancy mansion like you did, but that's by choice. Our work is in the hood, so we stay in the hood; we ain't forget where we come from. Except for Monk over there, who been trying to get all new on us lately. Don't judge a book by its cover; we're thorough. I can pick any lock. And I'm quick," Miss Cat said with pride. "I'm quiet and I've never been caught. You can't say that for yourself."

"And you already know about my driving skills," Nuquan said. "If anyone else would have taken that truck, you'd be in police custody right now. If you need to make a quick getaway, I'm your man."

"And what do you do?" Ebony asked Monk.

"I'm a businessman. That's all."

"Gimme a break."

"No, give us a break. You pay us three million dollars, that's one million each, and we'll help you get your money," Nuquan negotiated.

"Without getting caught," Miss Cat added.

"Hell, we'll even off the bitch for you and make sure they never find a body," Nuquan added.

"I told you, I don't even know if I have that much money left," Ebony said. "That could clean me out."

Miss Cat and her sons said nothing.

"What do you have to say about all this? You're just gonna extort me and not say shit?" Ebony asked Monk.

"I'm not looking to extort you. I don't think you're crazy. I believe you want to clear your name."

"Oh, you believe me? Well, gee, thank you," Ebony said sardonically.

"My brother and mother, although they're a bit over-zealous, are right. We can help you with just about whatever you need, but for a price. That's not extortion, that's just the way shit is. As for compensation, we'll work something out once you know how much cash you're working with," Monk said.

Ebony looked at Nuquan, Monk, and their mom.

What kind of people are these? Ebony asked herself. Then it hit her. They were *her* kind of people. She and her mother had been just like Miss Cat and her boys, partners in crime. The tears flowed before she could stop them.

Miss Cat had the same kind of hood swagger her mother had. Sure, Coco Knight had been more elegant and sophisticated with her diamonds, furs, and designer clothes, but she and Miss Cat shared the same essence. They were both out to get paid at any cost and were willing to bring their children into their hustle, whether or not that was the right thing to do.

There had been times that Ebony resented her mother for her high-speed, high-risk lifestyle. Sometimes she just wanted to be normal, or what she imagined to be normal. Sometimes she wished her mom had been a teacher or a secretary and that she'd been raised in a picture-perfect suburb rather than the gritty streets of Newark. Other times Ebony was grateful that her mother had given her some game and that she'd been able to flip that game into dollars. But mostly she just missed her.

"That bitch Carmelita killed my mother. She killed my man," Ebony said, choking back sobs. "She ruined my life."

"And you never snitched?" Monk asked her. "Not even after you got locked up?"

"I was raised to keep my mouth shut and to handle

my business on my own. Snitching isn't my style." Ebony dried her tears with the back of her hand and tried to be strong.

"The question I got to ask is, can you handle this?" Miss Cat asked. "You need some medication or something?"

"I told you, I'm not crazy."

"You better not be. If you fuck up, it's all our asses, and I'm not going to let nothing keep me from getting paid."

"Oh, I'll be fine," Ebony said, mustering a weak smile. *Everything isn't always what it seems, especially not me.*

Monk called his mother and brother into the living room for a quick sidebar.

"I'm a take the girl with me," Monk said.

"This ain't no time to be trying to get some pussy," Nu-Nu told him. "We trying to get paid."

"This is not about pussy. This is about business. I think that I'll be able to handle her better than the two of you. Y'all are too aggressive. I can tell she's on the edge of losing it. I'm gonna hold her together so we can get this payoff."

"We can hold her together," Miss Cat argued.

"Right. She jumped right out the window on y'all's asses. If I hadn't come back from walking the dog, she'd have been gone and her money would have been gone with her."

"I know you, Son. I can tell you like that girl, don't even front. As pretty as she is, you can't tell me you ain't feeling her," Miss Cat said.

"I don't know her so I can't say that I like her. I just think we'll get farther with her if we're nice to her. She's been locked up. I know how she feels," Monk said.

Nuquan shook his head in disbelief.

"A'ight," Miss Cat agreed reluctantly. "But, Monk, this broad is slick. Watch out for her."

"Y'all done talking about me?" Ebony asked when Miss Cat and her sons returned to the kitchen.

"Yeah, we're done," Miss Cat said. "I'm surprised your little ass ain't try to run out the back door."

"I thought about it, but that crazy-ass dog is out there. and he's bugging the fuck out."

Outside the dog could be heard barking and growling his head off.

"Monk, why the fuck is the dog barking like that?" Miss Cat asked.

"I'm gonna go see what's wrong," Monk said.

Before Monk could go out the back door, the barking stopped abruptly and the dog whimpered, then went silent. Monk froze in his tracks. He and Nuquan reached for their weapons simultaneously. Monk crept toward the back door and Nuquan slunk toward the front. Ebony felt a sick feeling in the pit of her stomach. Something was definitely about to pop off.

With a loud boom the front door was kicked off its hinges. Ebony immediately panicked. She dove out of her chair and underneath the kitchen table, shrieking as she heard the sound of glass breaking mixed with gunfire. This made the second time within a few hours that Ebony had found herself in the middle of a shoot-out. Ebony looked around frantically.

Miss Cat was crawling across the kitchen floor. When she reached the sink, she opened the cabinet underneath and pulled out a couple guns: a small pistol and a bigger, more intimidating hand cannon. Miss Cat slid the pistol across the floor to Ebony. For a moment Ebony stared at the gun blankly.

"Bitch, pick it up and use it if you have to!" Miss Cat yelled. "These motherfuckers trying to run up in my damn house!"

Ebony lifted the gun with trembling hands and scanned the room. She thought for a moment that she could shoot Miss Cat, Monk, and Nuquan in the head for putting her through so much shit but decided against it. Still, she had an opportunity. She took it. She ran as fast as she could down the corridor that led to the bathroom. She was going to jump out of the bathroom window again, and this time she didn't give a flying fuck about who or what was outside. If they tried to stop her from getting away, she was going to bust a cap in their ass.

She'd almost reached the bathroom. She could taste freedom. Then, a dreadlocked man appeared out of nowhere. Ebony didn't think and didn't hesitate. She squeezed off a couple shots. The man dropped at her feet.

Ebony was about to hop over the man and out the bathroom window when Miss Cat came running up behind her.

"Oh, shit!" she yelled. "Ebony blasted this fool!"

Ebony knew her opportunity to escape was the only thing going out the window. She dropped her shoulders and sighed.

"Damn, girl. Did you kill him?" Nuquan asked.

"Shit! Is we gonna have to call the police? I am not trying to call the police," Miss Cat fussed.

"We aren't calling the police, and we aren't going to stick around here either."

"I'm not about to let nobody run me up outta my house!" Miss Cat protested.

"Listen to me, Mama. It's not safe to be here. Nuquan totally underestimated the situation he got himself into. These motherfuckers are not playing around. I'm gonna take you and Nu-Nu to Aunt Pam's house. Do not let his ass out of your sight," Monk said.

"Monk, I'm a grown-ass man. I don't need no damn babysitter," Nuquan complained.

"Kill that noise. I'm not trying to hear it. Both of y'all do what I say. Mama, pack some clothes. Nuquan, go check the stash. Make sure it and the money is still where you left it. Then bring it with you. I'm gonna make sure these fools are gone. Then we're outta here," Monk said.

Ebony stood there while Miss Cat and Nuquan left to follow Monk's instructions.

"You, come with me," Monk told her.

Ebony looked longingly at the window. *So close, but so far away.*

CHAPTER ELEVEN

Miami, 6 p.m.

The man has been identified as Clyde Owens, age fifty-seven, a truck driver who was reported missing when he never arrived at his scheduled weekly drop-off for a plumbing-supply company in Sweetwater. Police have no persons of interest in his murder or the fire that destroyed his home, but foul play is suspected. Residents are being asked to call Crimestoppers if they have any additional information. And now we have a special report with Marisol Rivera-Frye."

Marisol flashed her colleague her pageant-winning smile. "Thanks, Tom." Then she turned to the camera with a serious expression. "Gross negligence may have been to blame in the fire at Everglades Psychiatric Hospital this morning. I've had a chance to talk to several employees, who described working and living conditions as deplorable, citing few working fire alarms, inadequate fire extinguishers, and no emergency escape plan in place. As reported earlier, three people are missing and presumed dead, and dozens more were transported to a local hospital, where as many as three patients are believed to have died from their injuries."

Rene Fields stood off-set and watched Marisol deliver her special report on the six o'clock news.

This is complete bullshit, she thought. *We've wasted an entire day on this crap and we're going to get scooped. Some other station is going to figure out what's really going on while we're here with our thumbs up our asses.*

Rene didn't want to hear about unqualified doctors, misdiagnoses, and fire safety. She wanted to get to the real meat of the story. She walked back to her desk and noticed that the message light on her phone was flashing. She entered her code and checked her voice mail.

"This message is for Marisol Rivera what's-her-name. My name is Jules Bratman and I'm an attorney in Miami Beach. I'm sitting here watching your story on Everglades, and I've got something you'll definitely be interested in. It's a letter from that broad, I mean that dame, you all did a story on, Ebony Knight. Call me." Jules left a contact phone number, which Rene promptly dialed.

"Marisol Rivera-Frye for Jules Bratman," Rene said, not bothering to clarify exactly who she was.

"This is him. You almost missed me. I was on my way out."

"I got your message about a letter from Ebony Knight."

"Yeah, strangest thing. It's been sitting on my receptionist's desk for days, but I just opened it today. I was thinking that you could have me as a guest on the news for one of your special reports. See, I'm a medical mal-practice lawyer and—"

Rene cut him off. "When can we meet?"

"I guess I could stick around my office a little while longer."

"I'll be there in fifteen minutes."

Rene scribbled a note telling Marisol she was gone for the day. She knew that Marisol was going to have a fit—Marisol didn't like her subordinates to leave before she did, even if they'd been there for twelve hours—but Rene didn't care. She gathered her belongings and hur-riedly left the station.

Although Jules Bratman had not been the most gallant of gentlemen when Rene spoke with him on the tele-phone, she was still surprised when she met him face-to-face. He was startlingly short, five feet five at the most. He was fat, bald, and had hairy knuckles. Nothing about him said lawyer, not even his expensive-looking but ill-fitting suit, which Rene could tell was new because he hadn't bothered to remove the label from the cuff.

"You aren't that Cuban dame," he said as soon as he laid eyes on Rene.

"No, I'm not. I'm her producer. She's at work on a story and can't leave the studio, so she sent me here to talk to you. She said you were a very important man," Rene said, stroking his ego. He stared at her breasts the entire time she spoke until she crossed her arms and cleared her throat loudly.

"I only ask one thing of you, Mr. Bratman," Rene said. "You're going to have to talk to my face, not my chest."

"Sorry, hon, but you're a knockout. I can't help myself. And you've got balls. I like that. Ya single?" he asked with a leer.

"I am very married and very happy, but Marisol is in the midst of an ugly divorce and she's looking for someone to help keep away the lonelies," Rene lied. "I'll make sure to send her your regards. Now, let's get down to brass tacks. Show me this package that you received."

Jules handed over a manila envelope that had photocopies of Ebony Knight's medical records. A handwritten note from her stated that the records were phony and that she'd never been seen by a Dr. Lawrence in New Jersey. Ebony also alleged that she'd been set up by her lawyer, Carmelita Sanchez, and that she feared her mother was in danger. She begged Jules to look into things and help her secure her freedom.

"So what did you find out?" Rene asked Jules.

"Find out?"

"Yeah. Did you find out if the records were forged? Was she set up by her lawyer? Did you ever locate the mother and talk to her?"

"It's under investigation," Jules said with a phony smile.

"So in other words, you don't know diddly and you haven't done squat."

"I called you, didn't I? Look, I'm not in the business of representing loonies or the dead. There's no money in it," Jules said with a sarcastic, rheumy laugh. "But you and Marisol on the other hand make a very good living digging for information. Consider this a gift. If you can't make it work for you, that's on you."

"And what do you want in return?"

"Well, unless you plan on cheating on your husband, you can't give me what I really want. But I'll settle for a spot on the news. Ya know, I can issue a formal statement. It'll be great for business, don't ya think?"

"How about this? I'll look into this stuff, and if this info leads to anything spectacular, I'll give you a call and a featured spot on a special report," Rene lied. She had no intention of contacting him again, but she had every intention of using the info he'd given her.

Rene returned to her modest apartment on South Beach and shucked her work clothes. Naked, she flopped onto her bed and pulled out her laptop. She googled Carmelita and looked at the images of her corporate headshot. *She doesn't look like a criminal mastermind. She looks like a model.*

Rene learned that Carmelita Sanchez had never lost a case when working as a criminal lawyer, but had since become a high-priced divorce attorney who specialized in seven-figure settlements. She also seemed to hobnob with South Florida's legal and philanthropic elite. Listed were all kinds of community service projects Carmelita had worked on and nonprofit boards she'd served on.

Hmm, pretty impressive. Seems like a stand-up kinda girl, Rene thought, inspecting a picture of Carmelita and a judge shaking hands with an inner-city youth at a scholarship benefit. *But people are never really who they seem to be.* Rene knew that the cleaner the public image, the more skeletons in the closet, was usually the case. There was only one way to find out. She had to talk to Carmelita Sanchez.

Rene decided to start at the heart of the allegations and dialed the law office where Carmelita practiced, even though it was past normal business hours. She was transferred to Carmelita's voice mail. She hung up and went back to her Web search to see if she could find anything.

"Bingo!" Rene said as she located the annual report of one of the charities Carmelita worked with. Her cell phone number was listed on the board-of-directors page. Rene blocked her phone number and dialed Carmelita. She didn't answer and the voice mail came on. Rene immediately called back. Still no answer. She tried one more time.

"Who is this?" Carmelita demanded as soon as she came on the line.

"I'm glad that I reached you. This is Kim, the receptionist at Dr. Lawrence's office in Newark, New Jersey. The doctor asked me to call you and get an address for Ebony Knight's doctor at Everglades in Florida."

"Who the fuck is this really?" Carmelita asked harshly.

"I told you who I am. The doctor heard about the fire

at her hospital and wants to be able to remain in contact with her counselors. You are Ebony Knight's conservator, aren't you? That's what I have listed here," Rene said innocently.

"That's bullshit! There's no way that happened. Now who are you?" Carmelita shrieked.

"Why do you say that there's no way that happened?" Rene probed.

Carmelita hung up.

Rene called the hospital Ebony was reported to have been treated at by Dr. Lawrence, Beth Israel, to try her hand at getting info.

"I was wondering if I could leave a message for Dr. Lawrence in psychiatry," she asked.

"I'm sorry but Dr. Lawrence in psychiatry passed away two years ago. Are you sure that's the doctor you're looking for?" the operator asked.

"There must be some mistake on my end. Thank you."

Oh, this is getting too good, Rene said silently. If her instincts were correct, she was on the verge of uncovering the biggest story of the year.

Carmelita Sanchez paced back and forth in her office. Her stomach churned and she felt light-headed. Somebody was onto her.

"Dr. Lawrence's office my ass!" she shrieked, stamping her foot. Her perfect plan was unraveling, and Carmelita felt a migraine coming.

Okay, calm down. There's an explanation and you've got to figure it out.

Carmelita rummaged through her oversize, white Chloé bag and pulled out a gold, engraved case. Damn her building's smoke-free policy, she was going to have a cigarette. She opened her window and looked out at Biscayne Bay while she puffed and thought. Even if someone had been digging through Ebony's case file and did learn that the medical records she'd used to have her committed were a forgery, the documents couldn't be tied directly to her.

She could always use Ebony's dead mother as a scapegoat. Only one other person knew what she'd done, and that was Amber, who had nothing to gain from telling anyone.

Nothing but millions.

Carmelita left her office and drove with haste to South Beach. As her car lurched in stop-and-go traffic, her frustration grew. Something was wrong and she was going to get to the bottom of it. Carmelita nearly rear-ended a taxi because she was so engrossed in thought.

"Get a fucking move on!" she yelled, laying on her horn. "Go!"

Finally Carmelita reached her destination, Amber's fetish store, Bound. Carmelita stormed through the front door and swept behind the counter and into Amber's office without bothering to say a word to the salesclerk.

"Hey, baby," Amber said cheerily upon seeing her lover.

"Hey, baby, my ass!" Carmelita yelled, slamming the door. "Who the fuck have you been running off at the mouth to?"

"What are you talking about?" Amber asked innocently.

"You know damn well what I'm talking about! The police came to see me today."

"The police? What did they want?" Amber frowned at Carmelita.

"They were asking a bunch of questions about Ebony."

"So what? You were the one who said you had things under control earlier, and now here you are in my place of business snapping on me as if I've done something wrong."

"I do have things under control," Carmelita said emphatically.

"So then what's this all about? You come in here all paranoid—"

"Fuck you, Amber," Carmelita said. "I'm not paranoid, I'm smart. We had one hell of a plan. I put a lot of effort into this shit. And in order to pull off something of this magnitude, you better question everyone and everything that could fuck you."

"And you think that I would fuck you?" Amber asked angrily. "After all that we've been through? That's real nice, Carm. If I remember things correctly, we've been in this *together*. We pulled this life insurance scam before without a hitch with *my* slave, remember? That's how

I got this store we're standing in. It wasn't until you brought in Ebony that things got fucked-up. You were so convinced she'd be down with the program."

"And she was."

"Yeah, right. If she was so down, why did the plan go so amuck? Why did *you* have to kill Erik Johansen instead of just blackmailing him for the big money, then arranging for him to have a convenient overdose like we planned?"

Carmelita glared at Amber.

"You can't say anything now, can you?" Amber asked smugly.

"I think that Ebony may have escaped," Carmelita blurted.

"Escaped?" Amber asked, then laughed. "You've got to be kidding me. You are losing it, you know that?"

"Well, the police think that the fire may have been to cover a botched escape attempt."

"*Botched* being the key word."

"Fuck that. I won't rest easy until Ebony's remains are in an urn on the mantel."

"Baby, why don't we just go home. I know something that will take your mind off things," Amber said suggestively.

Carmelita rolled her eyes. "Is that all you can think about? Have you not been listening to me?"

"I've been listening. And I'm not worried. You know why?"

"Please, tell me why," Carmelita said sarcastically.

"Because you're brilliant. All you need to do is release some tension and you'll figure out the answers to everything. You always do."

"I do, don't I?"

"Yes, you do."

Carmelita visibly relaxed, and Amber embraced and kissed her passionately.

"To be continued," Amber told her lover seductively, and they exited the store hand in hand.

"Well, will ya take a look at that," Rocky said as he and Marley watched Carmelita and Amber walk hand in hand to the Mercedes Carmelita was driving. "I can't believe a hot piece of ass like Carmelita Sanchez is into chicks!"

"I can," Marley said nonchalantly. "When the world is full of guys like you, its understandable that a woman would just give up altogether."

"Maybe you've got a little secret you're hiding," Rocky quipped.

"You know I'm happily married." Marley revved the engine and followed the Benz.

"Wonder where they're off to now."

"My guess is that they're headed to Ebony Knight's former residence."

"Why would they go there?"

"Because I know that Ebony Knight was telling the truth. And if Carmelita was trying to take Ebony's life from her and make it her own, wouldn't it make sense that she'd move into that big, beautiful mansion?"

"I guess," Rocky admitted. "But I don't know how anyone would want to live at the scene of those gruesome murders."

"Something tells me that Carmelita isn't the squeamish type. And you see the kind of joint they're walking out of. It's a fetish store. These women aren't afraid of mice or spiders or a little bit of blood."

"What makes you so sure?"

"Let's just call it women's intuition," Marley said as she tailed the couple.

Amber and Carmelita made a pit stop at a grocery store, and then, just as Marley had predicted, they drove down Collins Avenue until they pulled up to the Mexican-tiled driveway in front of Ebony's home.

"Now what?" Rocky asked.

"Now we wait. And watch."

"Great. An unexpected stakeout. I'm starving, Marley. Can't we get something to eat and come back?"

"Don't be a crybaby, Rocky. Here, have a nutrition bar." Marley reached across him and opened the glove compartment. "It'll tide you over."

"Bullshit," Rocky grumbled, then he angrily ripped off the foil packaging and took a frustrated bite of the granola bar. "Wonder what they're doing in there," Rocky said lecherously.

"You're such a perv. You know, women are more than

just—" Marley began, then noticed a woman walking with determination toward their squad car. "Busted."

"Can I help you officers?" Carmelita asked, her hands on her hips.

"No," Marley said with a terse smile.

"Would either of you like to explain why you're camped outside my house?"

"We're here on a police matter that is unrelated to you," Rocky said.

"Is that right?"

"Absolutely. It's a small world after all, isn't it, partner?"

"You got that right," Marley replied, slipping a pair of mirrored shades over her eyes.

Carmelita rolled her eyes and stalked away. She didn't know what the police were up to, but it didn't matter. *Those two flatfoots have no idea who they're fucking with,* she thought. Carmelita headed back into the house and straight for the telephone. It was time to call in a favor or two.

"Judge Berman," Carmelita barked into the receiver. "This is Carmelita Sanchez."

"Ahem, Ms. Sanchez, how are you today?" the judge asked, sounding flustered.

"Not so good. As you may know, my charge, Ebony Knight, perished in a hospital fire this morning at Everglades."

"I'm sorry to hear that."

"Save the sympathies, judge. You know I couldn't give less than a fuck about Ebony Knight dying, and neither do you. I think we both know why."

"I have no idea what you're talking about."

"Sure you do, judge. Your hand has turned the tide of justice more than once. You've helped me win a couple of cases in the past, and I've really appreciated your help."

"Carmelita," the judge said sternly. "What is it exactly that you want from me? She's dead, you've got your money, you got what you wanted."

"Not exactly. Now the police are sitting outside of my house."

"I don't know what to tell you, Carmelita."

"Oh, you'd better figure something out. Have you forgotten that I have all kinds of nasty little photos and videos of you in some very compromising positions thanks to my friend Amber? We may even have a few snapshots of you snorting a mysterious white substance off her boot while dressed in little pink panties," Carmelita said mockingly.

"You are a bitch, Carmelita."

"Yeah, I am. But so are you and not in the good way. If you don't want to fall with me, you'd better make sure that I don't fall. Am I making myself clear?"

"I'll take care of it," the judge said with a sigh.

Carmelita hung up and tried to relax. Good old Judge Berman. He was trapped and had no choice but to do what she wanted. Either the world would find out he was a freak and he'd lose everything he'd ever worked for, or he would play ball. Naturally he chose to play ball.

Carmelita had learned early on in her dealings as a lawyer at one of the city's most impressive law firms that wealthy and powerful men were really the same as other men. Their downfall was always simple, just as anyone else's: greed. The greed for money or the greed for pussy or both had taken down many a well-respected icon. That had been the way of the world since biblical days.

Practically every man Carmelita met in her business dealings hit on her, whether the men were married or not, and they thought she was dumb enough to try to sleep her way to the top. Carmelita used her good looks to her advantage, flirting with them, leading them on, then setting them up for a hard fall. It wasn't difficult to find out a man's weakness once you plied him with enough liquor. Carmelita knew that the key to getting what she wanted out of life wasn't in having the knowledge of influential people's freaky ways; the key lay in how she used that information.

She had at least three judges in the palm of her hand, and a couple senators, a mayoral aide, and countless corporate heads. For years she and Amber had worked as a team weaving a web of blackmail and power games, getting away with anything they wanted, including murder. Carmelita thought to herself that it was a shame things were coming to an end. She'd had a lot of fun. But the world was huge and people all over it were the same. There was lots more fun to be had.

★ ★ ★

Marley's cell phone rang five minutes after she and Rocky were spotted by Carmelita.

"Detective Parnell," she answered, not bothering to look at the caller ID. Her eyes were still firmly planted on Ebony Knight's home despite their having been cold busted.

"Get your asses back to the station," Captain Webster demanded.

"We're kind of in the middle of something."

"I don't care if you're in the middle of labor. Get in here now."

"Is something wrong?" she asked, but Captain Webster had already hung up.

"What's up?" Rocky asked.

"That was the captain, and he didn't sound happy. We've gotta go. Now."

"This is not good," Amber groaned after Carmelita hung up with Judge Berman. "Why the hell are the police sitting outside?"

"You're really driving me crazy, Amber. I swear you need to relax. Didn't you hear me on the phone with the judge? Everything is copacetic." Truthfully, Carmelita was just as worried as Amber, but someone had to at least appear to maintain her cool.

"It better be. We're in this together, baby. I mean, what if you're wrong? They're going to take my store, we're going to go to jail, they might even charge me as an accessory to murder. Carmelita, you were supposed to have this all under control!"

"Amber, shut the fuck up before I smack you in the fucking mouth," Carmelita growled. "All I'm hearing from you is 'me, me, me.' I can see from that bullshit you're talking that all you care about is yourself."

"It's not that, it's just that—" Amber was unable to finish her sentence or dodge the blow across her lips from Carmelita's fist.

"I said to shut the fuck up." Carmelita stood and dared Amber with her eyes to swing at her. She didn't.

"You really need to calm down. I told you I've got things under control and I do!"

"I'm sorry," Amber whispered, looking afraid. Carmelita laughed. It was amazing what a good pimp slap could accomplish.

"Look, baby, why don't you just try and relax. Go upstairs and run a bath while I open a bottle of wine. We'll have a little fun and then we'll get packed and go for a little trip for even more fun. You really should know better than to think that I wouldn't have planned for every possible outcome."

"Where are we going?" Amber asked.

"On a little vacation. We're going to Europe, baby."

"But what about the store?"

"Amber, relax. The clerk can run the store. So chill; everything's all taken care of."

"But don't we need passports or visas or something?"

"Amber, you're starting to bug me. I told you, it's all handled. You have nothing to worry about. Now run upstairs and get that tub going. I'm horny and I want you. I'll be up in a second with the wine."

Carmelita gave Amber a light kiss on the lips, swatted her playfully on the behind as she went upstairs, then slipped into the kitchen. From the wine humidor she extracted a bottle of Shiraz that she'd been saving for a special occasion. She got two crystal goblets from the china cabinet and went upstairs to join her lover.

"Here you go, babe," Carmelita said as she poured a glass of wine. Carmelita was about to hand her the glass, then reconsidered and put it on the bathroom counter.

"Let me look at you," Carmelita said seductively. She stroked Amber's milky white skin with her hand. "You're so beautiful."

"You're the beautiful one. I'm sorry I'm so spastic. I trust you, babe. And I love you."

"I love you, too. Now, Amber, you promised that you were going to relieve my tension."

"I sure am, baby. Sit back and relax, and let me help you get your mind right," Amber said.

Carmelita took off her clothes, allowing Amber to take in her perfectly toned, petite, golden body. Amber disrobed and they stood face-to-face. Carmelita reached out to caress Amber's large, full breasts.

"You have the best tits," Carmelita said, tweaking a rose-colored nipple before taking it into her mouth and sucking it gently. Amber sighed and stroked Carmelita's hair; Carmelita's free hand was busy between Amber's legs.

"Oh baby, you're so wet," Carmelita cooed, smiling at Amber.

"I'll show you wet," Amber replied, leading Carmelita to the tub.

The two women stepped inside the tub, kissing each other, the jets from the Jacuzzi swirling soapy water around.

"Sit on the edge," Amber requested.

Carmelita sat on the edge of the tub and opened her legs as Amber licked her, holding her lips open so she could have full access to Carmelita's clitoris. Water sloshed onto the floor as Carmelita spread her legs farther apart and pulled Amber's face closer, rotating her hips in small circles.

"That's right, baby, eat this pussy." Carmelita pulled Amber's hair and gave it a rough tug. Amber moaned and dove even more eagerly into Carmelita's pussy, using her tongue to explore her walls. Carmelita bit her lip and began to murmur in Spanish, standing in the tub and bracing herself against the wall. Amber held Carmelita's legs and knelt below her, her tongue rapidly gliding across her slick clit before taking the nub between her lips and nibbling it. Carmelita grabbed Amber by the throat and squeezed as she climaxed. Her shouts muffled Amber's gasps for breath as Carmelita clamped her thighs together tightly and ground her box against Amber's face.

As Carmelita shivered from the last throbbing sensations of her orgasm, Amber rose and kissed her passionately. Carmelita ran her tongue across Amber's lips, staring at her lustfully. Amber's raven tresses were wet and framed her catlike face.

"You're so fucking hot. That was so good," Carmelita said.

"Are you starting to feel relaxed?"

"Oh, hell yeah."

"Good. I've got an idea how you can get out any aggression you've been holding in. Maybe my little friend could join us." Amber smiled sweetly.

"C'mon, Amber. You know I hate that thing," Carmelita protested.

"Please," Amber begged.

Why not? This is the last time we'll be here together like this, Carmelita thought.

"Go ahead."

Amber stepped out of the tub and disappeared into the bedroom. She returned moments later carrying a huge strap-on dildo, licking her lips in anticipation as Carmelita stepped out of the tub and into the apparatus, securing it around her hips.

"You know, I don't have penis envy in the least," Carmelita said. "So I'm going to make you come the old-fashioned way first."

Carmelita backed Amber against the bathroom counter, and Amber hopped onto it.

"Do you want me to eat it?"

"Please, eat my pussy. That piece of plastic can never replace you. You're the best thing that ever happened to me. It's an honor to let me taste you and it will be an honor to feel your tongue."

"Amber, that's the best thing about you. You're crazy dramatic but you know how to totally submit to me. You've had so many losers kiss your ass and tell you how divine you are that you really know how to grovel. It's too bad your submission is only sexual."

"My submission to you is total."

"You doubted me."

"I was out of line. I apologize. Please, forgive me. You've always known what's best."

"I do. I know how to make the hard decisions, how to take the lead and not let emotions get in the way. Do you understand? You've never been on my level. I own you. You're my bitch." Carmelita stared at Amber, her lips curled into a sexy smirk.

"I'm your bitch. You own me. Totally." Amber was trembling. Carmelita didn't know if it was desire or fear, but she liked it. She threw Amber's legs open roughly and inserted a couple of fingers, sliding them in and out in a vibrating manner.

"Oh Carmelita, I love you so much. I'm so sorry I questioned you."

Carmelita moistened her lips and teased Amber's clitoris until she was begging for permission to come. Amber wasn't allowed to have an orgasm any other way.

"You can come. Come for me, Amber." Carmelita

smiled as Amber screamed in ecstasy. Then Carmelita mounted Amber with the strap-on and pounded her doggy style until they climaxed again. The entire time Carmelita watched in the bathroom mirror, making Amber watch as well.

"I could sure use that glass of wine now," Amber said, smiling at her lover's reflection. Carmelita handed Amber the glass of wine and watched as she drank it.

"That's good," Amber said with a smile.

"Well, then have another. I want you nice and re-laxed." Carmelita turned her back and poured another glass, but before she could turn around and hand it to Amber, she heard a loud crash. Carmelita calmly put the glass down, then swiveled on her heels to assess the damage. Amber lay on the floor on her side, her body twitching involuntarily. Carmelita flipped Amber's body over on her back with her foot. Amber's eyes fluttered and rolled around in their sockets, and her tongue dan-gled out of the corner of her mouth.

"That was so much easier than I thought it was going to be. I knew it would be fast, but I didn't think that fast. Cyanide is a motherfucker, ain't it?" Carmelita asked with a cruel laugh.

"Seriously though, I hate to have to do this to you, Amber," Carmelita said, crouching beside Amber and stroking her hair. "I really did love you. But you should have known that I couldn't let you live. You knew too much and you started to act weak, just like Ebony. And you know how greedy I am. I didn't want to share all that money with you. Hell, I didn't want to share it with Ebony, and it was hers."

Tears rolled down Amber's cheeks and she struggled to sit upright.

"Amber, save your energy. You're not going to find the strength to recover from this." Carmelita shook her head and stood. "You women who believe in love like it has magical powers make me sick. But I guess now you know that there is no such thing as love. Not between a man and a woman, not between two women, and not between a mother and child. People are selfish. Having warm feelings for someone doesn't change that. You had to learn the hard way."

Amber gasped for air and choked.

"Amber, right now the cyanide is keeping your vital organs from getting oxygen. You're fighting a losing battle. Death is inevitable, so prepare to meet your maker."

Amber shook and convulsed a bit before her body went rigid, then limp.

"Good-bye, Amber," Carmelita said before walking away from her lover's dead body.

CHAPTER TWELVE

Carol City, 4:30 p.m.

Ebony, Monk, Nuquan, and Miss Cat all piled into the stolen red truck that was stashed in the garage, and Monk drove a few blocks to 183rd Street. He turned into an auto repair shop and cut the engine. Monk got out and walked up to a group of muscle-bound men sitting in folding chairs in front of the shop. Seeing them together reminded Ebony of the old R&B group Full Force. The only things missing were arm-bands and Jheri curls.

She tried to listen to their conversation, but they spoke in muffled tones. Then Monk broke away from the group.

"Yo, Tika!" he shouted.

A butch-looking woman rolled herself from under-neath the car she was working on and walked over to the group.

"Tika, I'm a need you to take care of this truck." Monk tossed her the keys. "Then you can go on home. We're not gonna be open tomorrow, but don't worry, you still gonna get paid for the day."

"Cool! You got it, boss," she said, and left.

"Come on," Monk told Ebony, leading her into an office and shutting the door behind him. "You want something to drink? I got some bottled water and Coke."

"I could use a Coke," Ebony said, looking around. "What is this place?"

"What's it look like? It's my office."

"Office?"

"Yeah. Don't most business owners have an office in their place of business?"

"You own a garage?"

"Among other things. I'm not a multimillion-dollar mogul like you but I do all right."

Ebony was impressed. "Wow, you're an entrepreneur. And here I thought you were a hustler."

"Not the kind that you're probably thinking about. I got out of that game a long time ago, but I didn't forget how to play it. I'll still get my hands dirty every now and then, but for the most part I'm trying to do something new."

"It's hard to get out the game. Sometimes I think you're never really out. It's a whole lot easier said than done," Ebony said.

Monk went into a little refrigerator behind his desk. He handed her the cold can of soda and their fingers brushed against each other's. Ebony locked eyes with Monk and held his gaze. He smiled.

"Yeah. You're right about that." Monk walked away and dug in his desk drawer.

If I didn't know any better, I'd swear dude is checking for me, Ebony thought, unable to suppress a grin.

Monk pulled out a set of keys. "Let's go."

The group caravanned in a black Tahoe out to Pembroke Pines to drop off Nuquan and his mother at her sister's house before Ebony and Monk headed back toward the city, riding in relative silence. Making small talk was far from her mind. Ebony was plotting her next escape attempt. It wasn't that Miss Cat and her sons were that bad, although drama seemed to follow them. Ebony could respect their hustle, and she knew that they could possibly help her. But her vendetta was best accomplished on her own. It was personal.

"I have to apologize for what happened back at the house. My mom and brother have a way of getting caught up in drama that I end up having to fix. But they aren't really as crazy as they seem," Monk said, his baritone voice finally piercing the silence.

"Oh, yes, they are," Ebony disagreed. "I was minding my own business when your brother came crashing into my world."

"You aren't exactly Polly Purebread."

"I never said I was. But I don't fuck with people who don't have it coming to them. Unlike your brother and your mother."

"You can rest assured that the man that ran up in my mom's crib had it coming. And you can believe that we all appreciate what you did back there. We could have all been killed. So thank you."

There was an awkward silence.

"You know, I can't picture you as a mental patient," he said, smiling and shaking his head.

"I find that hard to believe. Didn't you see all the media coverage of my tawdry scandal? It's been the talk of the town for a few months." Ebony rolled her eyes.

"I don't really watch much TV."

"Do you read the newspaper? Because as far as I know, my picture and all kinds of details of my life, some true but most of them not true, were splashed on the pages of just about every tabloid and newspaper around."

"I especially don't read the newspaper."

"Don't you want to know what's going on in the world around you?" Ebony asked, thinking to herself that she sounded like Miss Cat scolding Nuquan earlier.

"I don't need a bunch of propaganda to tell me that. I've got two ears and eyes of my own and a bunch of common sense. Besides, I feel very connected to the world."

"How very Zen of you," Ebony said sarcastically.

"That's why they call me Monk," he said with a chuckle.

"Really?"

"No, not really. It's short for *Monkey*. When I was a little boy, I used to like to climb all over shit. Then I ended up fixing cars, so I guess it's short for *grease monkey,* too."

"Well, it's a lot better than Fuquan, that's for sure," Ebony said wryly.

"Hey, I know my name is a little different."

"Nah, it's not. It's your typical hood name."

"No, actually it isn't. It's Chinese. My pops liked kung fu movies. My brother and I both have Chinese names. Nuquan got the raw end of the deal. His name means 'women's rights.' My name means 'master fist.'"

Ebony gave Monk a look, and they both burst out into hysterical laughter.

"I didn't say my dad actually knew what the names meant in Chinese when he named us. He just didn't make them up," Monk explained as he chuckled.

"Oh my God! I needed that laugh."

"You're one to talk about names. Ebony Knight? Can we say made-up?"

"I'll have you know that is my birth name."

"Yeah, right."

"I'm serious. My mother's name was Coco, and she wanted to name me something along those lines."

Monk laughed some more.

"Yeah, I guess it was kinda corny, huh?" Ebony asked as they pulled into a parking garage beside a loft building in the design district.

"You live over here?" Ebony asked, looking around.

"Yeah."

"My business was in this neighborhood," Ebony said wistfully. "Before it and everything else I had slipped through my fingertips."

"What happened?"

"I can't believe you don't know. Come on, let's go

inside and go online. I can show you better than I can tell you."

Ebony and Monk went inside his loft.

"This is a nice spot," she said as she walked around admiring the contemporary furnishings and artwork that adorned the walls.

"Thanks." Monk led her to a neatly organized teak desk. "My computer's over here."

Ebony sat down and logged on to her website.

"Once upon a time I was a dominatrix," she explained as she navigated through her site, pointing out pictures and descriptions of her business. "And not just any kind of dominatrix. My specialty was financial domination. Men paid me to basically financially fuck them over, and they got off on it. I engaged in all the typical S-and-M stuff, but I did it for a very, very high price."

"That sounds suspect. Like a high-price prostitute."

"I never, ever, fucked my clients," Ebony said, her face serious. "Fucking for money doesn't show any domination, power, or control. I had total control. I dictated to my clients when to eat, sleep, fuck, jack off, you name it. I ran the show. I called the shots."

"And people paid you for that? Sounds like a wife to me."

Ebony laughed. "Yeah, it's pretty crazy-sounding, I know. But most people have fetishes. You kind of have to take a walk inside their minds to understand why."

Ebony typed in the Web address of the *Miami Herald*. She entered her name into the search bar, and an archive of articles about the murders of Erik Johansen and Jeff Cardoza popped up.

"By the time I figured out why my best client, Erik Johansen, had the proclivities he did, it was too late. He was in too deep. I don't care what you read here, I'm telling the truth when I say that I never had any intention of him dying. He made me filthy rich. He paid me three thousand dollars per session, bought me a car, real estate, gifts. I flipped what he did for me into an empire of my own that made a pretty penny. In a twisted kind of way I was grateful to him for putting me on. It's not totally his fault he was imbalanced. That man, that wealthy, powerful man, had a more fucked-up upbringing than you could ever imagine. His father used to beat the shit out of his mother and even tried to kill him. Finally his mother couldn't take it anymore. She killed him."

"Damn, that's deep," Monk said.

"That's not where it ends. His mother started sexually abusing him, and he eventually killed her. It was unintentional but he just never recovered. He was able to carry on with business; I guess throwing himself into his work along with seeing me was cathartic to him. But once I knew what happened, I couldn't keep on seeing him. It felt wrong. But he wouldn't let go. He stalked me. He threatened my life, and my fiancé Jeff's life."

"I'm still missing some pieces here."

"Well, my best friend, Carmelita, she was the one who got me started in the whole dominatrix scene. She introduced me to a woman called Goddess Amber, who owns a fetish store on the beach, and she referred Erik to me. In hindsight I can see that it was all a setup. Carmelita helped me with the legal aspects of taking Erik's money, funneling the funds through the proper channels and whatnot. Once I told her about Erik's past, she got it in her head that we could blackmail him to keep quiet.

"I didn't want to do it. But he pushed me to the limit, you know. He made my life miserable. I figured making him lose ten million dollars would get him off my back."

"It didn't?"

"Nope. It made him more obsessed. He nutted up and tried to kill me and my man. Carmelita actually saved our lives. She killed Erik. She tried to get my fiancé to go along with things but he wouldn't, so she killed him, too. I was really freaked out, but we made a pact to protect each other. I was lucid enough to do that. I went to the mental hospital for observation and didn't say a word about what really happened. Carmelita was supposed to get me off in exchange for claiming that I killed Erik in self-defense after he killed my Jeff. But she reneged on her end. She framed me and left me to rot in Everglades while she took over my life. Then, as if that weren't bad enough, she killed my mother. Mama was all that I had left." Ebony started to cry. "If I could just go back, things would be so different. I would have never trusted Carmelita."

Monk rubbed her back while she cried. Ebony let go. She released the floodgate of the emotion that had been pent up inside her, emotion she thought she'd already let go but that she discovered still lingered.

"I don't know what to say," Monk told her. "I wish I could tell you something that would make you feel better, but I can't."

"I know this is going to sound really crazy. I mean, I don't even know you. But can you just hold me? I haven't had a hug in months, and I swear if I don't feel someone's arms around me this second, I'm going to fall apart." Ebony looked at Monk through tear-filled eyes.

Monk didn't reply, he just opened his arms and pulled Ebony in. Ebony closed her eyes and inhaled deeply as she felt Monk tighten his grip around her. She laid her head on his chest and listened to the rhythmic thumping of his heart. Monk softly stroked her hair as they stood in the middle of his living room holding on to each other.

Ebony stopped crying and looked up at Monk. "This is nice."

"Yeah, it is, but—" He tried to break their embrace.

"But what? We're both adults. And if my instincts are correct, we both want more than to just hold each other."

"Ebony" was all Monk could manage to say. Her lips were on him, kissing his mouth and neck. Her hands roamed over his body, caressing his shoulders and running down his back. She didn't stop until her hands were gripping his ass. She pulled him closer.

"Don't you find me attractive, Monk?"

"Hell, yeah."

"Don't you want me?"

"I do."

"Then I don't see why you're hesitating. I need you. I need you in so many ways. I need you to help me. Help me get my life back. Help me be strong again. I know that if I can feel you inside me, I'll feel human again. I'll know what I need to do," she murmured, nipping Monk's earlobe with her teeth.

Ebony let her hands travel from Monk's ass around to the front to caress his crotch.

"Oh, I can feel that you want me." Ebony gripped his erection in her hands. "Stop trying to resist it."

Monk held Ebony at arm's length, staring into her toffee-colored eyes. "You are so fucking pretty. But you're dangerous."

"I'm not. Not anymore. I'm vulnerable. And I need you."

Ebony stepped back and pulled off her T-shirt. She removed her bra and caressed her breasts.

"Touch me," she instructed Monk, guiding his hand to her chest. Monk was hesitant at first, letting his hand hover above her bosom.

"Monk," Ebony seductively whispered. "Touch me."

Monk couldn't hold back. Grabbing her full, firm breasts with his hands, Monk bent down and flicked his tongue over her dark areolas and erect nipples.

"That's right," Ebony encouraged him. "Just like that."

Monk worked his way from her breasts, up toward her collarbone, grazing her clavicle before gliding his tongue up her neck. He nibbled her ears, his breath feeling warm against her skin before he darted his tongue inside. Monk grabbed Ebony's face in his hands and kissed her forcefully. Their tongues danced in and out of each other's mouth as Ebony stripped out of her remaining clothing.

"Take your clothes off," she breathed huskily, then watched as he peeled off his jeans and boxers and stood in front of her naked. Monk's body looked as if it were made of chocolate marble crafted by a master sculptor.

"Got a condom?" she asked as Monk's hands stroked her swelling clitoris.

"I'll get one."

Monk retrieved one from a drawer in his desk and put it on. Then he lay her on the floor and entered her roughly. Ebony opened her legs wide, allowing him to penetrate her deeply.

"Girl, you feel so good. Too good," Monk said as his hips moved back and forth like a piston.

"So do you," Ebony replied, before wrapping her legs around him to pull him in farther. "You stroke this pussy so good."

Monk moaned as he increased the speed of his thrusts. Ebony could feel him growing closer to a climax.

"Not yet. It's been so long. Turn over."

Monk did as Ebony asked, flipping onto his back without withdrawing his throbbing member from her dripping box. Ebony ground her hips, slowly at first, increasing her speed as the sensations between her legs grew stronger and stronger. She looked down at Monk, running her delicate hands over his chiseled chest.

"You're sexy as hell," she murmured.

"So are you!" Monk muttered, beads of sweat forming at his brow and rolling down the sides of his temples.

Once again Ebony felt his body tense; he was on the brink of climax.

"I told you, not yet!" she said, lifting herself from his cock. "I need you to hit it from the back," Ebony told him after he'd calmed down a bit.

Monk entered Ebony from behind, holding on to her shoulder as he guided himself inside her tight tunnel. It took them a second to synchronize their rhythm, but when they did, the results were heavenly. Ebony rocked her hips in time with Monk's thrusts, supporting her weight on her elbows, arching her back so Monk could push himself as deeply within her as possible. Ebony's body began to quiver and she couldn't suppress her screams.

"Oh, Monk, I'm coming," she moaned as the walls of her pussy began to twitch and throb.

He grabbed a handful of her hair and pumped his hips in a frenzy before groaning and climaxing.

"That was . . . dope," Monk said after they'd disengaged their bodies and tried to catch their breath.

Ebony laughed. "Yeah, it was, wasn't it?"

"Hell, yeah. Girl, you put it on me. Let me take a little nap, and then whatever help you need, you got it."

"Sounds good to me."

Ebony watched Monk as he drifted off. She watched and waited until she thought he was asleep. Then she threw her clothes on, grabbed Monk's car keys, and slipped out of the apartment.

CHAPTER THIRTEEN

Rene Fields entered Carmelita Sanchez's name into ZabaSearch and took out a pad and pencil. Only two Carmelita Sanchezes were listed for the entire state of Florida, one in Lake Worth and the other in Miami Beach.

"Women really ought to be way more careful these days," Rene said. "If this is her, then it was way too easy to get this info."

Rene put on a pair of camouflage pants, a tank top, and a baseball cap. She had a small spy-cam built into an ink pen, which she'd purchased to catch her doggish ex-boyfriend cheating, and figured that it would come in handy. She stuck the pen behind her ear and smiled at her reflection in the mirror.

By this time tomorrow, Marisol is going to be yesterday's news, she thought.

After stopping at a Chinese restaurant for a pickup, Rene drove to Miami Beach and parked her car in front of an art-deco-styled building. She walked past the tele-phone entry system straight to the front door. She was immediately buzzed inside and walked up to the security desk.

"Yeah, I got a delivery for Sanchez," she told the uniformed guard in a fake New York accent. There was really no need to disguise her voice, but it gave Rene a rush. She felt like a real reporter rather than an assistant.

"Sanchez?" the guard asked with a chuckle. "Which one? We have a couple of them."

"Carmelita Sanchez."

"No, you don't have an order for her," the security guard said, shaking his head.

"W-what do you mean?" Rene stammered.

"I mean you've got to be mistaken. She doesn't live here anymore."

"Hmm," Rene said pensively. "I don't know what could have happened. She called in with her regular order and this is the address on file."

"She moved a while ago. You can use my phone to call her if you like," the guard offered, pushing the phone toward her.

"Her number isn't on the receipt, unfortunately. We've got a new girl taking orders and she forgot to write it down. She's not that bright, and if I call in, she won't be able to retrieve it from the computer system for me. My boss is going to have my ass if I'm late with another delivery, and I really need this job. What am I gonna do?" Rene asked, pouting and stamping her foot, her breasts undulating underneath her tight T-shirt.

"I don't know what to tell ya," the guard replied, seemingly unfazed by Rene's jiggling and bouncing.

"You wouldn't happen to know where she lives now, would you?" Rene asked, poking out her chest some more and biting her lip.

"It's against policy for me to divulge that kind of information."

"Oh, please, do you think you can help me out?" Rene asked with a sexy grin. "I'd love you forever if you did." Rene stroked the security guard's cheek playfully.

He finally cracked and smiled a mile wide. "For a pretty girl like you I'll make an exception. But you'd better not tell anyone I did this," the guard warned, wagging his finger at her.

"I swear, your secret is safe with me." Rene crossed her heart with her finger.

The guard opened a notebook sitting on his desk and flipped through some pages. "She left a forwarding mailing address." He pushed a slip of paper toward her with an address scribbled on it.

"You're an angel." Rene blew the guard a kiss and skipped out of the lobby.

Rene could barely see straight as she drove, she was so excited. She dug in the bag and pulled out an egg roll. Munching on it, she mapped out her next steps. Smiling to herself, she thought about how her first foray into investigative journalism had started off with a bang. She'd got hot information and followed her leads doing whatever it took to bring her closer to breaking an exclusive story. She was not only proud of herself for being brave enough to take a risk, even if it could possibly jeopardize her job, but was gratified that the risk seemed to be inching closer to a reward.

But Rene began to get the jitters by the time she reached the address. She'd played out a dozen different scenarios of what she was going to do. She considered pretending to be one of Ebony's relatives needing information about her funeral but decided to stick with the food-delivery routine since it had already worked. She just wanted to make sure that Carmelita let her in; once she was inside the house, she'd figure out a way to learn what she needed to know from Carmelita, and she'd record it all on the pen camera. Rene took a deep breath and rang the doorbell. There was no movement inside the house. Rene rang it again.

"Who is it?" Rene could hear the irritation in the woman's voice.

"Delivery."

"I didn't order any delivery. You must have the wrong address."

"No, ma'am. The ticket says this address. Is there a Carmelita Sanchez here?"

The door swung open and a woman stood glaring at Rene. "I'm Carmelita."

"Your Chinese is here," Rene said with a smile.

Carmelita smiled back. "Hmm. Well, even though I didn't order it, it smells delicious. And I didn't cook. So it looks like this is my lucky night. How much is everything?"

"Fourteen seventy-five."

"Come in. Wait right here while I get my wallet."

Rene stepped inside the foyer and marveled at the beach home. *Maybe I am in the wrong fucking business! I should have been a dominatrix.* She watched Carmelita go upstairs, thinking that she looked sweet, not at all like the monster Ebony described in her letter to Jules. Rene put the food down on an end table, activated the camera, and tiptoed into the living room. She didn't see anything out of the ordinary.

"This is a really nice house you've got here," Rene called out. "I'd have to work ninety years to afford anything like it."

Carmelita didn't respond. Rene crept back to the foyer. Moments later Carmelita came downstairs holding a $20 bill. Rene reached out to take it. Carmelita grabbed Rene by the wrist and twisted her arm behind her back. Rene struggled, nearly overpowering Carmelita until Carm pushed her face-first against the wall. Hard.

"What the hell?" Rene wrestled her arm free from Carmelita's grasp and whirled around. She was face-to-face with the barrel of a gun.

"Who the fuck are you?" Carmelita hissed.

"I'm the Chinese food–delivery girl." Rene looked at Carmelita with doe eyes.

"Bullshit! Who sent you?"

"The restaurant."

"I just called the restaurant. They don't have any delivery orders for me."

"We've got a new girl who keeps screwing every-thing up."

"Uh-uh." Carmelita shook her head and backed Rene up to the wall. "I recognized your voice. You're the woman that called me asking about Dr. Lawrence this afternoon. So unless you want to have your head blown clean off, you better start talking. Who the fuck sent you? Was it Ebony?"

"I don't know any Ebony. I swear!"

Carmelita scowled at Rene. "Fine. Have it your way." She hit Rene upside the head with the gun.

Can either of you explain to me why I just got a phone call from the chief of police about two of my officers violating a civilian's right to privacy?" Captain Webster asked Marley and Rocky when they returned to the precinct.

"Are you serious?" Marley asked.

"Dead ass," Captain Webster said.

"We weren't harassing anyone," Marley said. "We questioned Ebony Knight's attorney, Carmelita Sanchez, at her office."

"We didn't like her answers, so we followed her. I don't know how she made us," Rocky said.

"And that fact that she did make us is beyond the point. We're well within our rights to keep persons of interest in a federal crime under surveillance. Why did the chief get involved?"

"I don't know why he got involved, but he's involved. I've been told in no uncertain terms that Carmelita Sanchez is off-limits. So stay away from her," Captain Webster told them.

"Damn, does she have that kind of juice?" Marley asked.

"Apparently so," Captain Webster said. "You're just going to have to find another way to get to the bottom of things."

"Don't you find this suspicious?" Marley asked.

"Extremely," the captain said. "Sanchez has something to hide, and the powers that be are helping her hide it. But there's nothing we can do. So please tell me that you got something we can use."

"We talked to one of the staff doctors at Everglades who treated Ebony Knight and Kira Long. She asserts that Ebony Knight didn't belong in the hospital. She says that the lawyer is the one behind Erik Johansen's murder. Ebony claimed that the lawyer forged court documents in order to frame her."

"Do we believe the maybe-crazy lady and her shrink?" the captain asked.

"I do, now more than ever. We'll make some phone calls to verify it, but I'm pretty sure of what we're going to find. Carmelita is well connected. I don't know to whom, but she's got some serious pull. She managed to get us off her back. There's no telling what else she's gotten away with," Marley said.

"And I'm still on the fence," Rocky said. "I'm not

totally convinced that Carmelita and Ebony weren't working together."

"What about the roommate?" the captain asked.

"The doctor says she's as dangerous as they come. Unfortunately the doctor has no idea where she might be headed. She suggests going to the media."

"I don't want this going public just yet. You've got until the morning to find these women. Otherwise, be prepared for a press conference," the captain informed them.

"And a flood of phone calls to the Crimestoppers hotline. We all know what that means," Marley complained.

"Yeah, a whole bunch of bogus information and wasted time chasing leads from here to Albuquerque," Rocky said.

"Well, you know what you have to do," the captain told them.

"So what do you want to do, partner?" Marley asked Rocky after they left Captain Webster's office.

"I want to get something to eat and go to bed, that's what I want to do."

"You know what I mean. You want to go back to Ebony Knight's house and find out what's really going on with Carmelita Sanchez?"

"I do, but you heard the captain. We can't go near her. We may as well get ready for that press conference. I'm getting too old be pulling all-nighters. Besides, I'm hungry," Rocky whined.

"You sound like a bitch," Marley said, irritated. "Come on and let's get something to eat."

Marley and Rocky settled into a booth at a twenty-four-hour Latin diner on Mid Beach and ordered two Cuban sandwiches and fries. Marley rolled the paper wrapper of her straw between her fingers while she waited for her food, a pensive look on her face.

"So what do you think is going on?" Rocky asked. "I can see the wheels turning in your head."

"You know what I think, Rocky. I think Carmelita Sanchez set up Ebony Knight and is the real killer of Erik Johansen. Why else would she be so secretive?"

"Well, most people don't take too kindly to the cops sitting outside their home, especially after being questioned."

"You mean to tell me that you still think that Carmelita is clean? Are you serious?"

"Nah. As much as I hate to admit it, I think you're right. Not wanting the cops outside your house is one thing, but getting the chief of police involved is another."

"Yeah, I wonder who she's got in her pocket," Marley mused.

"Doesn't matter right now. We can't go near Carmelita, and we still have the matter of Kira Long on the loose to take care of."

"Man, fuck Kira!" Marley exclaimed, pounding her

fist against the table. "You heard that doctor. We're never going to find her. We'll just have to deal with the inevitable shitstorm that follows a press conference. For now I say we go back to Ebony's house and keep watch."

"What good would it do? As much as I want to see what those two lesbos are doing, I doubt that we'd be able to find anything that we could use in court."

"Rocky, its not politically correct to say *lesbos*," Marley scolded.

"I'm not politically correct."

"I know. Which is why I can't understand why you want to sit here and play the role of a stand-up cop. You're always down to break the rules."

"Marley, I'm hungry and we've been on the road all day. There's a time to break the rules and there's a time to be patient and wait for a break in the case. You've gotta look at the big picture. We can't fuck this up on a technicality. Any other suspect and I'd be with you. But Carmelita is crafty. We really need to watch our step with her."

"I know, you're right, but I want to nail this bitch so bad!"

"I knew you were a lesbo," Rocky joked.

"Har har," Marley replied sarcastically. She was just about to lay into Rocky when her phone rang.

"It's the captain," she told Rocky as she looked at the caller ID. "I wonder what we're in trouble for now?"

"I'll get it." Rocky took the phone away from her. Marley shrugged and doused her remaining fries with ketchup before shoving them in her mouth.

Rocky muttered intermittent *uh-huh*s, *yeah*s, and *gotcha, boss*es before hanging up Marley's cell and giving it back to her.

"Let's roll," he said, leaving the remainder of his sandwich on the table as he got up and headed to the door.

"Oh my God! You left food behind," Marley said, feigning shock. "What can the captain have possibly said to make you do that?"

"We've got the break we need."

"Someone's found Ebony?"

"No, but we've been able to pin down Kira Long's location. She went to her parents' house. They're stalling her, but we've got to move!"

When Rene came to, her hands had been handcuffed behind her back, and she was sitting in a chair next to the dining-room table. She blinked her eyes and attempted to focus on the owner of the voice that spoke to her. Carmelita was holding the pen camera in one hand, a gun in the other.

"Got any last requests?" Carmelita asked, pointing the gun at Rene's forehead.

"Look, this is all just one big misunderstanding. If you'll kindly point that thing in another direction, I will explain it all to you."

"Misunderstanding my ass. I understand perfectly. That bitch Ebony sent you, didn't she?"

"I don't know anyone named Ebony."

"Oh, come on, Rene. You expect me to believe that?"

"How did you know my name?"

"I looked at your driver's license."

"Good. Then you saw my work ID, right? I work at Channel Seven."

"I saw it. It's just like Ebony to get some starry-eyed sucker with prime-time dreams to take up her cause. What did she promise you? Your name in lights? An exclusive interview? Money?"

"I don't know what you're talking about."

"Then who sent you from your station? What are you planning to broadcast about me?"

"We're not planning anything. Call the station. I work for Marisol Rivera-Frye."

"Why did the glorified weathergirl send you here? To do her grunt work? Is that bitch behind this?"

"Marisol didn't send me. She doesn't even know that I'm here."

"Well, that's good to know. Now I have a little insurance that no one is gonna come looking for you here. But I'm growing a little impatient with asking you the same question over and over again. So either you tell me who sent you, or I'm going to have to resort to some unpleasant methods to find out." Carmelita flashed a sinister grin.

"What do you plan on doing with me?"

"If I like what I hear, perhaps I'll let you live. But if I don't, I'm going to kill you."

"The police will investigate."

"I'm not worried about the police. You're the one who talked her way into my house with Chinese food. Now talk, or your pretty little face is history."

Carmelita pulled the hammer back on her gun.

"Okay, okay. I got a tip," Rene offered quickly. "Actually the tip was for Marisol, but I took the info and investigated it myself without telling her. Ebony Knight sent someone a letter from Everglades. In it she said you framed her for the murder of Erik Johansen and that you killed Jeff Cardoza and her mother. I was just following the lead, trying to get my big break."

"Who did she send the letter to?"

"Some ambulance chaser."

"Which one?"

"Jules Bratman."

"That hack?" Carmelita turned up her nose.

"He doesn't know shit. He didn't even bother to check the info in the letter. He was just trying to get his fifteen minutes of television fame."

"Is he the only one with the letter?"

"I don't know."

"Did you show it to anyone or talk to anyone about it?"

"No."

"There's still a problem though, Rene."

"What? I've told you everything."

"Yes, but you know everything, too. That lawyer might not have investigated things, but you sure did. That's why you're here. You know that Ebony was never seen by a Dr. Lawrence in Newark. You know I forged her medical records."

"But it's not what I know, it's what I'll talk about. And I'm not saying shit," Rene swore.

"Do I look stupid to you? Do you think that I believe that?"

"It's the truth. I'll leave town. I'll leave the country. I'll do whatever you need me to do. But please, let me live," Rene begged.

"Just tell me where the bitch is. Is she outside? Is she waiting for a signal from you?" Carmelita peeked out the drapes.

"I'm telling you, I acted alone. I swear to God!"

"I don't believe in God."

"I swear on whatever you believe in. Please, I just want to go home. I'm sorry I bothered you."

"I'm still going to have to kill you. I'm thinking self-defense will get the police off my back."

Rene began to cry. Everything had gone horribly wrong.

"Carmelita. Think about what you're saying. I'm a nobody. I'm not worth all this trouble. If you let me go, I swear I won't tell anyone anything. Besides, that excuse is going to start to wear real thin with the DA. Think about it, Carmelita. Twice in this house someone was murdered in self-defense. It's never going to fly."

"It'll fly. See, I'm more powerful than you'll ever know. I have friends in high places as well as low, and I utilize them all. This gun I'm holding is stolen. I got it from a real shady character who needed my help. There's no telling how many bodies are on it. I'll just have to tell the authorities that it was yours, that we struggled and that I overpowered you. It'll add up."

But maybe it won't, Carmelita thought as she paced the floor. Things were really getting out of hand. She couldn't let Rene live, but killing her would be messy. As it was, she still had to dispose of Amber's body. Also, Rene had a point. If Carmelita killed Rene and then called the police, they were going to be mighty suspicious of another self-defense case at Ebony's house. Then it hit Carmelita. There was a way to make it all disappear, one that made plenty of sense. She'd have to adjust her plans a bit, but it would probably work.

"Come on, let's go," Carmelita said.

"Where are we going?"

"Your house."

CHAPTER FOURTEEN

M en are so predictable," Ebony said as she scurried to the parking lot as quickly as a rat darting across a New York City street. She laughed as she disarmed Monk's car alarm and got inside.

"I can't believe this makes twice in two days that I've been able to make a getaway in a stolen car because someone couldn't hang after getting a little pussy."

Ebony thought about the security guard that her former roommate Kira slept with. She'd been banging him for who knew how long, but their little indiscretion was the key to freedom. Literally. While he was busy getting his rocks off, Ebony was at work removing his keys from his uniform pocket. This time pilfering keys had been just as easy but far more enjoyable.

"The dick was good," she admitted to herself as she drove out of the parking lot. "Real good!"

Ebony's eyes gleamed with self-satisfaction as she raced Monk's car toward her destination: her old home. Ebony was willing to bet her kidneys that Carmelita was staying there.

It won't be long now. You're going to get what's coming to you.

The car suddenly and drastically slowed down. Ebony checked the gas gauge. The tank had plenty of petrol.

Her eyes flitted about the dashboard. No warning lights were illuminated. She pressed down on the accelerator with no results. The car continued its deceleration.

"What the fuck is going on?"

Ebony panicked. The car's roaring engine was muted to a purr, and she was certain that if she jumped out of the car and started running, she'd sprint past the vehicle faster than a member of the Jamaican track team in the Olympics. She was going to do just that, but a tow truck pulled up alongside her and rolled its window down.

"Ebony! What the fuck are you doing?" Monk screamed from inside.

Ebony tried the gas again. Nothing happened.

"Ebony, you may as well pull over," he yelled. "You're not going to be able to go any faster."

Ebony sucked her teeth and pulled over to the side of the road. Monk did the same and approached her with his teeth gritted. He rapped on the window.

"Get out the car!"

Ebony crossed her arms and shook her head.

"Fine, then I'll just hook this shit up and tow it with you inside."

Ebony opened the door, nearly hitting Monk in the legs as she did.

"How you just gonna fuck me and then steal my car? You must really be crazy!" Monk grabbed her by the shoulders.

"Because I've been trying to tell you and your family all day that I have shit to do that I have to do on my own. But, no, you all just insinuate yourselves into my vendetta and basically extort me for some help that I didn't ask for and that I don't need." Ebony freed herself from his grip. "And how the hell did you find me?"

"GPS antitheft system. I tweaked a LoJack to alert me instead of the police."

"Who the fuck are you, the damn Knight Rider?"

"Girl, come on."

"I'm not going anywhere with you!" Ebony yelled.

"Ebony, I can understand that you're pissed off, but you need to recognize when somebody is trying to help your ass."

"Why the fuck would you help me? You don't even know me," Ebony hissed.

"You got money and I'm trying to get paid."

"So that's what this help is about?"

"Ain't that enough? You just told me all the crazy shit you did to get millions, but you can't understand where I'm coming from? I'm trying to get enough money to get out the game and get my moms and lil' brother out the hood," Monk yelled.

"Oh, God! What is this, *Menace II Society*? It is not my responsibility to get you and your fam out the hood."

"You're right. But the way I see it, we got a chance to help each other out. That's the problem with black folks. Always tearing each other down and never reaching out."

"Listen to yourself. You sound bananas. This ain't no time for Black Love. Understand what I'm trying to do. I'm trying to kill a bitch!"

"And I'm trying to stop you from making a big mistake. You may think that you want revenge, that you want to take this Carmelita chick's life. But trust me, you don't want her blood on your hands. Once you got a dead man's blood on your hands, it never washes off."

"I know. I've already got plenty of blood on my hands. I'm prepared to deal with a little bit more."

"You think so, huh, tough girl? Okay, fuck it! Have it your way. You out for blood, then come on. I'll take you anywhere you need to go." Monk threw his hands in the air in frustration, then shoved Ebony into the tow truck he was driving.

"What about the car I took? Is it going to be okay? You gonna hook it up to the tow truck?"

"Don't even worry about it. It'll be fine. Where do you need to go?"

"I'm pretty sure that Carmelita is chilling at my house, but just in case we'll swing by her condo."

Ebony directed Monk to Carmelita's place. Aside from an occasional "Turn left" or "Keep straight," they didn't speak. When they arrived at their destination, Ebony said, "I need you to wait here. If I'm not back in ten minutes, you can dip."

"Whatever." Monk didn't even bother looking at her.

Ebony got out of the car, walked to the gate in front of the building, and looked at the electronic directory. Carmelita's name was no longer listed. Ebony picked up the telephone next to the directory and dialed Carmelita's old access code. Ebony heard a disconnection message and hung up. She headed back to the waiting car and driver.

"Let's go." She gave him the address of her home.

Monk shook his head as he drove Ebony toward her old home.

"Put this on," he said, tossing her the baseball cap he was wearing.

Ebony tucked her hair behind her ears and put on the cap, pulling the brim down low over her eyes. Her hands began to shake the closer she got.

"Is that it over there?"

"Yeah, that's it." Ebony's eyes welled with tears as she looked at her home. She hadn't expected to be so overwhelmed when she finally made it here, but it had been so long since she'd seen it and she had so many memories here. She remembered when her and Jeff's cars were the only ones in the driveway and half expected Jeff to come walking out the front door to scoop her up in his arms and tell her that he loved her and that they'd never be apart again. Now Amber's candy-apple-red vintage Porsche sat in front of her once happy home along with Carmelita's BMW and Ebony's Mercedes.

"That bitch has been riding in my whip and living in my house off my money like it's hers. This shit comes to an end now!" Ebony said bitterly.

"Well, go on then. Go on your one-woman mission to kill a bitch without so much as a butter knife on you," Monk said, his voice sarcastic.

"I've got plenty of knives in the house," Ebony retorted, holding back her tears.

"So, what, you're in the fucking circus now? You plan on throwing knives at the bitch? You're ridiculous. Get out my damn car." Monk was clearly heated.

"There's probably a gun in the crib, too," Ebony said, even though her ride had given her the boot.

"Probably. Well, good luck with your 'probably.' Like I said, get out."

Ebony didn't move. She couldn't. She wanted revenge, but something was holding her back.

"I had a real nice piece before . . ." Ebony's voice trailed off.

"Before what?"

"Before Carmelita used it to kill my Jeff."

"I see." Monk threw a knowing look in her direction.

Ebony couldn't restrain herself anymore. She started to cry hot, angry tears. Her breath was rapid-fire and her chest heaved. Monk turned away until she shut off the waterworks.

"You okay?" he finally asked.

"I'm fine. I'll be all right," she said, trying to pull herself together.

"So what you waiting for? Go on and kick in the door and kill Carmelita and the other bitch in your crib with your bare hands."

Ebony said nothing.

"You can't, can you?" Monk turned her face toward

his. "Ebony, I feel you, you want to get even. I can only encourage you not to use violence as a solution, but if that's what you feel is your only option, then do what you gotta. But at least do it right."

"What would you know?"

"Look at me, Ebony. You think a body like this comes from working out at the gym? I got this build from lifting weights in jail. I been locked down before on some bullshit, and I know how it feels to want to pay a motherfucker back. I also know that it's never worth it in the end. Now come on back to my crib. We'll get something to eat and then you can plan to make your next move your best move."

Ebony nodded in agreement, angry at herself for being such an emotional wimp. She and Monk traveled back to where they'd left his car and hitched it to the tow truck, then drove back to his place.

"You know before your ass cut outta here in my whip, I was going to tell you that I'm pretty sure I can get you your money without you even having to go through the bullshit you trying to do," Monk told Ebony once they were back at his place.

"How can you do that?"

"My mother and brother are into the more street-level crime. I keep telling them that's not the way to go. When I get my hands dirty, it's white-collar. I'm nice with the computer."

"You're a hacker?"

"Yep. And I'm tight. If your girl has an online bank account, I can get in, get your cash, and transfer it to a new account in minutes."

"Are you serious?" Ebony asked in shock.

"Yeah. Dead ass."

"Why didn't you just come out and say that then?"

"You distracted me," Monk said, smiling.

"Well, get undistracted. Handle that."

"You know what bank she uses?"

"Probably still the Swiss one we set up when we got the money."

"Come on." Monk walked to the computer.

Ebony hesitated. "Wait."

"What?"

"I changed my mind. I just want to do things my way. I need to have the satisfaction of my face being the last thing she sees before I kill her. I know I punked out back there, but I will get it together. And when I do, I'm going to kill that bitch."

"I'm sure you will. But that's not the reason you won't let me do it. You don't trust me, do you?"

"That, too. I mean, how do I know you aren't going to take all my money?"

"You don't. So have it your way if that's going to make you feel better."

"Are you still going to help me? I'll need a ride back to my place once my mind is right, and it would be nice to know that someone has my back, just in case."

"Yeah, I'm still going to help you. And you're still

going to pay me. Don't even think about fucking me over either. Because I will find you and fuck you up, no matter how good that pussy is," Monk said, smiling.

Ebony laughed. "You think I got some good pussy, huh?"

"Yeah, you do. But you ain't about to use it to try and get over on me again."

"I know I can't use it to get over on you again. But I can use it for a more positive purpose." Ebony walked over to where Monk was sitting at his computer and straddled him. She leaned close to him and looked him directly in the eye. *Hell, I may as well get some more dick while I'm trying to get my mind right,* she thought.

"What you got in mind, girl?" Monk asked, grinning.

"Like I told you earlier, I can show you better than I can tell you."

"Then show me."

Ebony grabbed Monk by the throat and kissed him deeply. He kissed her back with equal passion, then stopped abruptly. He lifted Ebony from his lap and onto the desk, laying her flat on her back and spreading her legs. Then he was on her again, grinding his hard cock against Ebony's crotch. She moaned with every stroke, feeling herself growing more and more aroused.

"Is that pussy wet?" Monk breathed in her ear.

"Oh, hell, yeah! But you can make it wetter."

Monk pulled Ebony's pants off and practically ripped her panties off. "Can I eat it?"

Ebony nodded and closed her eyes, opening her legs

wider to accommodate his broad shoulders. Monk spread her lips apart gently and licked her slowly. Ebony shuddered and almost came on the spot; she hadn't felt a tongue on her clit in so long. Monk flicked his tongue across her swollen button with gentle, delicate strokes before burying his face in her pussy. His tongue was everywhere, lapping, licking, nibbling over her inner lips and clitoris. Ebony moved her hips rhythmically, luxuriating in the sensations.

"Damn, Monk, that feels so fucking good."

Monk slipped a long, thick finger inside her and wiggled it around slowly. He slipped another one in and worked his hand slowly, looking up at her to determine what she enjoyed the most.

"I want you to come for me," he told her in a husky voice.

"I'm warning you, it's going to get really messy."

"Let go, girl. Let it all go. Give it to me."

Ebony felt her entire body tingle and tears stream down her face as she thought of Jeff and how he used to make her come the exact same way. The mixture of pleasure and heartbreak was bittersweet and powerful, and Ebony's body thrashed on top of the desk as she screamed in ecstasy. She felt her juices streaming down her thighs as Monk continued to lick her and work her box with his fingers. Finally, when Ebony stopped bucking and shouting, Monk climbed on top of her and kissed her. She could taste her muskiness on his lips and tongue.

"It's going to be okay," he told her, stroking her face. "We're going to make it okay, baby."

Ebony looked up into his eyes and couldn't understand why a man she'd met only hours earlier was being so sensitive, but quickly resigned herself to the thought that some things had no explanation and succumbed to the lust and desire she felt. Monk reached in the desk drawer for another condom and rolled it onto his thick, meaty cock. Ebony sighed as he entered her, stroking her slowly when she needed it slow and faster when she needed it. The entire time he told her he would be there for her, reassuring her that everything would be fine, until finally neither of them could contain themselves. They fucked fast and furious, gripping each other tight, papers and supplies flying off the desk and falling on the floor.

When they were done, they held each other, looking into each other's eyes but not speaking. Finally Ebony broke the silence.

"Monk."

"I know. You have things you need to do."

"As much as I would love to lie with you like this all night, I have business to tend to."

"Of course."

"Plus the stapler is wedged in the crack of my ass!" she said with a hearty laugh.

"You liked it, too," he said, laughing back.

They climbed off the desk and got dressed in silence.

"You know, Monk, I loved my man, I really did." For

some reason she felt the need to explain herself, but she wasn't quite sure why.

"I know. But there's no reason to feel bad about this, and there's nothing that you need to explain. You needed it, I needed it."

Ebony nodded. "How come you don't have a girl? That is, if you don't have a girl."

"I had one. But she wasn't trying to do the same things as me. She still wanted to be in the streets. Since her, I haven't met anyone who held my attention long enough for me to make them my girl. Now, you ready to do this?"

"Yeah. As ready as I'll ever be."

"All right, then let's go get your money."

While Monk drove Ebony back to her old home, she pumped herself up for the task ahead. She thought of all she'd built and all she'd lost at the hands of Carmelita. The bitch had to pay. The bitch had to die.

"I'm going to park out front. I'll ring the doorbell and distract her while you let yourself in the back door. When she opens up, I'm just gonna rush her from the front. You rush her from the back," Monk said when they got near her house.

"Fine, sounds like a plan. But whatever you do, make sure that you don't kill her. Leave that to me."

"I got rid of the gun you had in the truck. But here's a

piece for you." Monk handed her a gun. "Think you can you handle it?"

Ebony examined the gun. "I should do okay."

Ebony checked to make sure the safety was on, then put it in her waistband.

"If I hear shots before you let me in, I'm kicking the door in."

"Cool," Ebony said. "Let's go."

She got out of the truck a ways down from her house and walked along the section of private beach that lined the townhomes on her street. When she reached hers, Ebony peered inside the patio door that led to the kitchen. She had an unobstructed path of vision from the kitchen to the living-room door thanks to the open floor plan and didn't detect any motion or hear any noise. She could hear Monk ringing the doorbell. There was nothing. He rang again. Still nothing.

That's odd. All the cars are out front. Where could she have gone?

Ebony reached in her pocket and pulled out the set of spare keys she'd got from the safe-deposit box and quietly let herself inside. Ebony crept across the kitchen, her eyes darting around for any sign of Carmelita. As she eased into the living room, she could hear the faint sound of the television upstairs. Ebony walked to the front door and let Monk in.

"Is she home?" Monk whispered.

"Not sure. You check downstairs. I'm gonna try upstairs."

Monk slunk around the lower level of Ebony's home while Ebony went up the stairs. She padded silently across the carpet and slipped into the bathroom en suite.

Carmelita is about to get the shock of her life. I'll sneak into the bedroom through the bathroom and get her ass, Ebony plotted silently.

Ebony certainly wasn't prepared for the gruesome sight in front of her. She screamed at the top of her lungs.

Monk came running into the room, his gun drawn.

Ebony stood in the middle of the bathroom, her hand over her mouth. In front of her lay Amber's dead body.

"Is that her?" Monk asked.

"No. This is Amber."

"Who do you think did this to her? Carmelita?"

"It's possible," Ebony said, unable to take her eyes off Amber's corpse. "I wouldn't put anything past her."

Ebony stopped staring at Amber's dead body and looked around the room.

"I don't think Carmelita is here. There's a half-packed suitcase on the bed," Ebony said, pointing at it. "But her car, Amber's car, and my car are all out front."

"What do you want to do?" Monk asked.

"If she comes back, I'll be here waiting for her, but in the meantime let's go down to my office and see if we can get our hands on my money."

"Oh, you want me to hook that up now?" Monk asked, grinning.

"Yeah. Trusting you is a chance I'm going to have to take. For all I know Carmelita could be gone for good."

They went downstairs and Ebony made sure all the curtains and shades were closed and the doors were locked. Ebony looked around as she walked through her home, her fingertips touching the walls, the drapes, the furniture. She thought she could still smell Jeff's cologne but knew her mind was playing tricks on her. Everywhere she looked there was a memory. The kitchen where she and Jeff used to cook dinner, the living room where they used to dance, the foyer where they'd shared their first kiss.

Ebony had been away for two months and things seemed familiar yet foreign. Everything was practically just as she'd left it, but the little things, such as a vase in a slightly different spot, or a picture frame turned in another direction, made her feel as if she were walking through a stranger's home.

"This is a nice-ass crib. Makes my shit look like a shack," Monk said.

"It's nice all right, but it doesn't feel like home anymore. This will never be home again."

Monk followed Ebony into her office. When she took a seat at her desk, a wave of fury hit her. Carmelita had her own framed photograph perched on the desk where a picture of Ebony, her mother, and her father had once been. The screen saver that once bore a picture of Ebony and Jeff was replaced with a picture of Carmelita and Amber. Ebony gritted her teeth to prevent herself from kicking her desk over. Ebony picked up the picture frame and hurled it against the wall.

Monk just looked at Ebony. "You okay?"

"Fuck no!" she screamed. "I can really see what's going on now. The two of them were totally in it together. They took everything from me and played me like I was some kind of game."

"It's going to be all right."

"No, it isn't. It isn't ever going to be all right again. My mama and Jeff were the only people who ever loved me. That's gone now."

Ebony paced back and forth.

"Ebony, you can't keep focusing on that. Keep their memories in your heart, but eventually you're going to have to let go of the anger. It's the only way you're going to be able to move on. I'm not saying it's going to be easy or that it won't take a long time. But it will happen. Now, Ebony, focus on what we're here to do. You can't get your mama or your man back, but you can get your money. Now sit down. Let's do this. Let's see how smart this Carmelita really is."

Ebony gave Monk the Web address of the Swiss bank that they'd used to launder the blackmail money they'd extorted from Erik Johansen. His fingers danced across her computer's keyboard, the furious clicking sounding like the taps of shoes hitting concrete. Ebony watched in wonderment as he bypassed the log-in page and accessed Carmelita's account.

"Is this it?" he asked, turning the flat-screen computer monitor toward Ebony.

"That's it. Shit! How did you learn to do that?"

"Some I taught myself, the rest I learned from a white cat I was locked up with. He taught me what he knew in exchange for protection."

"What were you locked up for?"

"Maybe one day I'll tell you the story behind all that. For now, let's figure out what to do with this money. I can complete a wire transfer to another account. Do you have one you want to use, or you want me to set up a new one?"

"You'll have to set one up. Then go on and wire three million dollars to your account."

"I'm not going to take your money, Ebony."

"Are you nuts? After all that trouble this afternoon, now you don't want it?"

"I want it. It just feels weird to take it."

"The feeling will pass. Do it."

Monk shrugged. "You ain't gonna have to force me to take it."

Monk typed some more before turning to her and saying, "Done."

"So that's it?"

"That's it. See, your numbered account is here." Monk pointed at the screen, then scribbled on a sheet of paper. "This is the log-in address and this is your temporary password. You can change it now if you want to, if that would make you feel better."

"What's the point? If you really wanted it, you'd probably be able to get it."

"Is that your way of saying you trust me?"

"Something like that."

The sound of a cell phone made them both jump.

Monk laughed. "It's me."

Monk took the call. Ebony watched his smile disappear like the sun behind the clouds during a thunderstorm. Monk furrowed his brow and a vein on the side of his head throbbed and bulged. He muttered a few words and hung up.

"What's the matter?"

"That was one of those Jamaican cats that got beef with Nuquan. They've got my mom and brother."

"What do you mean they've got them? As in kidnapped?" Ebony asked, her eyes widening.

"Yeah. I don't know how they found them, but those motherfuckers done run up in my aunt's crib," Monk said through gritted teeth.

"Oh my God. Is everyone okay? What do they want?"

"It's a long story."

"What are you going to do?"

"I'm gonna do what I gotta. It looks like you're going to get your wish; you get to handle your revenge against Carmelita on the dolo. You're on your own. I gotta get out of here and get to them."

"Of course, man. Family first."

Monk nodded.

"Good luck, Monk. And thank you for everything."

"You know, it isn't too late for you to walk out the door with me. You don't even know if this chick is coming back."

"I'm going to have to take my chances and wait," she replied with a determined look in her eyes.

An awkward silence.

"You know, maybe in another life me and you could have had something," Monk said.

"Maybe. In another life." Ebony smiled at him.

"I guess I'll see you next lifetime."

"I guess so."

Monk kissed Ebony on the lips, then headed out the front door.

CHAPTER FIFTEEN

Miami, Midnight

Marisol was beyond heated when she realized that Rene had left without permission.
She stalked around the newsroom like a
tyrant, fussing and cussing at anyone who looked at
her sideways. For over four hours Marisol attempted
calling Rene's home and cell phones and left dozens
of messages, escalating in anger and abusive language
until she couldn't take it anymore. How *dare* someone
ignore her? Well, she wasn't going to let some peon of
an assistant get away with playing her. Marisol went to
confront her.

"She'd better have a damn good excuse for cutting
out on me like that," Marisol said to herself as she drove
to Rene's apartment. She was tired of taking shit from
assistants that weren't as committed to their jobs as she
was to hers. She didn't care that it was after midnight.
Rene had some serious explaining to do if she wanted
to have a job to go to in the morning.

"Rene! Open up! I know you're in there! I saw that

piece of shit you call a car parked outside!" Marisol yelled as she banged on Rene's front door. There was no answer. Marisol kept thumping on the door.

"Excuse me, miss. Do you know what time it is? I'm trying to get some sleep. You're going to have to cut out all that racket!" A middle-aged woman with curlers in her hair had stepped out of her apartment and was standing in the hall, her hands on her hips.

"Do you know the woman that lives here?" Marisol asked, ignoring the neighbor's request.

"Who, Rene? Yes, I know her. She's a lovely girl. And usually so quiet. She watches my cats when I'm away visiting my granddaughter in New Jersey." Then a look of recognition spread across the woman's face. "Wait a minute! Aren't you that reporter from Channel Seven? The one she works for?"

"That's me," Marisol said, smiling with pride.

"She said you were a piece of work." The woman sniffed her disapproval at Marisol and began to walk back into her apartment.

"She said what? Wait a minute, lady!" Marisol yelled.

"My name is Mrs. Rosenberg, not lady. And I don't work for you, missy, so I'd appreciate some respect!"

Marisol took a deep breath. Maybe she was taking the wrong approach with the neighbor. She softened her tone.

"I'm sorry, Mrs. Rosenberg. I'm just very frustrated right now. You see, Rene left without telling me and I need her help on an extremely important story," Marisol lied.

"Maybe she had an emergency. Rene isn't the type of person to leave someone when they need her. She's very responsible. A lovely girl."

"Yes, she is lovely. She's such a help to me. That's why I'm so desperate to find her. Have you seen her tonight?"

"I didn't see her, but I heard her come in. Didn't hear her go back out. Maybe she's in the shower. Did you call her?"

"I did. I called her cell phone and her home phone. There was no answer on either."

"Maybe she has a gentleman caller and doesn't want to be disturbed."

"I don't care!" Marisol yelled. "I don't care if she's in there with Jesus, if she wants to keep her job, she'd better *open the damn door!*" Marisol punctuated her sentence with a loud thwack on the door.

"I've tried to be nice to you, young lady, but I think you'd better leave. This is a quiet building. We don't need or want all this."

"Mrs. Rosenberg, I know that I'm disturbing you, but I'm not the type to back down. I didn't get to where I am by being easily intimidated. Now I need something, so do what you have to do, but I'm not leaving until I speak to Rene. And just think, no one will be able to watch your cats if Rene can't afford to pay her rent because she's lost her job. Or what's worse, think about how bad you'll feel if something is wrong with her."

"What do you expect me to do?"

"Is there a super around? Someone who could open up so I could see if she's at home?"

"We don't have a super."

"What about your key? I'm sure you have one."

"It's for emergencies only."

"This is an emergency. A news emergency. Do you think you can just pop your head in?" Marisol pleaded with a sweet expression on her face.

"I'm not a nosy old busybody. What if she's in the act? You know? A little hanky-panky."

"Mrs. Rosenberg, you'd be doing me such a huge favor, not to mention helping the young lady you know keep from blowing the best opportunity of her career. And I would be more than happy to show my gratitude. I happen to have a pair of tickets to the Barbra Streisand concert. Third row. They're yours if you help me."

Mrs. Rosenberg went into her apartment and came back immediately with the keys to Rene's place.

"Normally I'd never do anything like this, but the Barbra show has been sold out for months."

Mrs. Rosenberg knocked before slipping her key in Rene's lock and turning the knob.

"Rene, honey, it's Martha from next door." Mrs. Rosenberg peeked her head in and entered the apartment a step at a time. "Rene, honey?"

There was a bloodcurling scream.

"Rene! Rene, oh my God!"

"What's wrong?" Marisol barged in.

Rene lay in bed, a bottle of pills in one hand, a note on the bed next to her.

"Something's wrong," Mrs. Rosenberg said.

"You don't say."

"I mean, Rene would never do anything like this. She was a Christian girl, a Catholic. Very devout."

"Catholics commit suicide."

"Rene wouldn't. She had very strong beliefs. We talked about things. Also she was a happy, sweet girl. The only problem she ever had was dealing with you and your work drama, but even so, she had no reason to do this. Call the police."

Marisol ignored her and picked up the suicide note.

"*Good-bye*? That's it? Now that is strange. Rene was not a one-word kind of girl."

Mrs. Rosenberg folded Rene's hands across her chest and frowned. She bent over and put an ear to Rene's nose and mouth. "I think she's still breathing."

"I don't think so," Marisol said.

"Get over here and see for yourself."

"I'm not going anywhere near a dead body."

"I'm telling you, this one isn't dead!" Mrs. Rosenberg picked up the phone herself and called the authorities.

"Your friend is going to make it. She's unbelievably lucky. It's lucky for her that OxyContin is time-released.

If you'd waited any longer, she would be dead. We're going to keep her for observation, run a couple of scans to make sure that there's no brain damage. And of course she's going to have to be examined by a psychiatrist. But, you can see her now," a doctor in a white coat explained to Marisol.

"Rene, what the fuck? Was working for me really that bad?" Marisol asked when she entered Rene's room.

Rene nodded yes, then laughed a dry, listless laugh.

"You bitch!" Marisol muttered.

Rene grabbed Marisol by the collar and pulled her close. Her stomach hurt from having it pumped and her voice was hoarse.

"Marisol, I didn't try to kill myself, especially not because of you. Someone tried to kill me and make it look like a suicide," Rene whispered.

Marisol looked at Rene as if she'd said she was queen of the giant cluck-clucks. "I can't believe I hired a nutcase," Marisol said under her breath.

"Marisol, listen. Do whatever it is that you need to do to get me out of here. I mean right now!" Rene screamed, then raised her hand to her throat.

"Why would I do that? You clearly need help." Marisol looked at Rene with pity.

"What I have to tell you is going to get you that Emmy you want so bad."

"Go on." Marisol stood back and flashed Rene a dubious look.

"There's only one catch. You're going to have to share it."

"With who?"

"With me."

Marley and Rocky arrived at the Long residence at the same time as the fire department.

"Shit!" Marley exclaimed as she slammed the car into park.

"Please tell me we're not too late," Rocky pleaded as he rushed to the house faster than a running back headed toward the end zone, and with just as much determination.

They were stopped by a fireman. "I'm sorry but I can't let you go past here, Officer."

"Have your men checked for bodies?" Rocky asked.

"They're already on it."

Moments later a crew of men exited, wheeling out two bodies covered with black plastic bags.

"We've got a man and a woman," one of the crew yelled.

"Fuck, fuck, fuck!" Marley stamped her foot like a tempestuous two-year-old. "I know those are the parents."

"Any possible chance there's one more body inside?" Rocky asked the fireman.

The fireman got on his radio briefly. "I'll let you know in a second."

"She got away! The crazy bitch got away, I know it!" Marley screamed in frustration.

After some time the fireman informed them that after a thorough search of the smoldering home, no more bodies were found. He also said that the fire was not the probable cause of the Longs' deaths.

"The bodies are only slightly burned. We caught the fire pretty early. I'm no medical examiner, but I can tell you that both of them were stabbed. The father's neck was practically severed."

"Damn! She did that to her own parents?" Marley asked.

"This broad really is as demented as the doctor said she was," Rocky said, shaking his head.

"So now what?" Marley asked.

Rocky rubbed his temples. "So now we go home. It's after midnight. We've been on this case all day. I'm tired, I'm cranky, and there's no way we're going to find Kira before the press conference in the morning. The parents were our best shot at catching Kira, and its doubtful she had any other friends or family that would help her. Our trail is cold and I don't intend on chasing any more fires."

"I know that you aren't giving up on me like that, are you? Just because we can't get Kira doesn't mean that we can't get Ebony Knight," Marley said.

"Marley, I don't share your obsession with Ebony Knight."

"I'm not obsessed. I just know that I'm right."

"Yes, you *are* obsessed. You have been from the start.

This isn't one of your husband's crime novels, Marley. Besides, don't you have to get home to him?"

"My husband understands how important my work is to me. He supports me. He's got my back, unlike you at the moment. Besides, he's probably pecking away at his computer. He's got a deadline. Now come on, let's go back to Ebony's place."

"And do what? Lose our badges from fucking with someone that's got way more power than us? It's just not worth it," Rocky said.

"We're not going to lose our badges if we crack the case."

"Marley, not all of us have rich and famous husbands to support us. Some of us are the breadwinners of our households."

"Rocky, why can't you see what's right in front of you? Ebony Knight is more than likely on one of two missions. She's either gotten good and lost and we're never going to find her, or she's going to go after Carmelita to get revenge. My bet is on the second one. For all we know, Ebony could be there right now. Think about it! Ebony's lost everything: her mom, her man, her career, her home, her money, and her freedom. She's not the type of chick to just lay it down, not by a long shot. She wants revenge."

"Marley, why can't *you* see what's right in front of you? I'll admit that I think Carmelita Sanchez is dirty. But what I don't understand is why it never occurred to you that maybe the two of them were in it together from the beginning. Maybe Ebony hated her mother, and maybe she and Carmelita are both lesbians and Ebony doesn't give a shit about Jeff Cardoza being killed. Maybe he was always expendable. Ebony probably set the fire to escape and fake her death, and Carmelita is probably planning to go and meet her and split up Erik Johansen's insurance money as we speak. It was all a big scam. That's why Carmelita got so damn defensive about us sitting outside her house. She doesn't want to chance us tailing her when she meets up with Ebony."

"You're wrong," Marley said. "You're dead-ass wrong."

"Marley, there's no sense in standing here arguing. I'm going home. I suggest that you do the same."

Marley and Rocky rode back to the precinct, where Rocky got into his car and left.

"I don't care what Rocky says. I'm going to get to the bottom of things," Marley muttered as she turned in the keys to the unmarked Crown Victoria and got into her Toyota Avalon.

Rene told Marisol the story of how she'd tracked down Carmelita Sanchez and was forced to swallow a bottle of painkillers or have her face blown off.

Marisol couldn't believe her ears. "We've got to go to the police. This woman is psychotic!"

"I agree, but first we've got to go back to that house!" Rene said.

"You can't be serious. For what?"

"For the exclusive. Plus my pen camera is still there.

We've got evidence, we just have to get it. No other station even knows what's going on. We've got proof. Imagine Carmelita's face when she sees that her plan to kill me didn't work. It'll be priceless."

"No way! This time she might just shoot us both on sight. I just can't take that kind of chance," Marisol said. "It's a job for the cops."

"She won't shoot us. Not with a camera pointing in her face."

"You have no way of knowing that."

"No, I don't. But are you going to let an Emmy slip through your fingers? Through our fingers?"

Marisol didn't answer.

"Plus, Carmelita is convinced that Ebony Knight is on the way to kill her. She got real chatty when she was driving me back to my place to fake my suicide. She told me that she was planning on skipping town. We've got to get back to the house before Carmelita leaves."

"I hear you, Rene, but there's no way I'm letting you leave in your condition. I'll handle it, but I'm going to handle it my way. The right way. I want to make sure I live to tell the tale."

"How do I know you're not going to try and take all the credit for breaking this story?"

"You have my word."

"Not good enough. I want it in writing."

Marisol scribbled a promissory note of sorts, swearing that she'd credit Rene as a producer and coanchor.

"Is this good enough?"

"It'll have to do," Rene said, and they both signed the paper. "I don't want to hear any bullshit from you later saying that I wasn't of sound mind and body when I signed this," Rene threatened Marisol in a scratchy voice.

"What kind of person do you think I am?"

"I work for you, Marisol. I know exactly what kind of person you are."

"Well, obviously you don't know me as well as you think that you do. You know, I used to have my doubts about you, Rene. I honestly didn't think that you had what it took to make it in this industry. But I believe in a little while, you and I are going to be each other's fiercest competition."

Rene rolled her eyes and made a face at Marisol.

"Seriously. You put your life on the line for a story. Not many reporters would do that. I'm not even sure that I would do something like that. I respect you, Rene."

Rene smiled. "I never thought I'd say this, Marisol, but I respect you, too. Thanks for giving me this opportunity."

Marisol thought to herself that the things she said to Rene were partially true. She did respect Rene's ambition. But mostly Marisol felt that she had no choice. Rene could have one hell of a lawsuit on her hands if she wanted to. Marisol figured that appeasing Rene would be the best thing to do for everyone involved.

"I still think I should go with you," Rene said. "Someone should have your back."

"Look at you. You can barely walk and talk, so I'm going to have to be the one who confronts her."

"Be careful, Marisol. Carmelita Sanchez is dangerous. She's killed before, and as you can see from my predicament, she has no problem killing again. I went in there on a solo mission and it almost cost me my life."

"No worries. I'll call the cops because that bitch is absolutely going to pay for what she did to you. And she's going to have to pay for leaving me without an assistant for a couple days. But first, I'm going to stop at my house and get my gun. I'll be ready for her. "

"You have a gun?"

"Not only do I have a gun, I know how to use it very well. I've got a concealed-weapons license and everything. Rene, this industry has its bad along with its good. There are a lot of weirdos out there that think they know me because they see me on TV. I can't be too careful. And as you see now, neither can you."

Rene nodded.

"Before I go, I'll talk to your doctor. You're probably still going to have to talk to a counselor before you leave, but I doubt that you'll have to stay any length of time for a psychiatric evaluation."

"You sure you're not gonna pull a Carmelita Sanchez on me? I'd hate to wake up in a mental hospital because you forged my medical records," Rene joked.

"I promise I won't. I still can't believe she did all those things."

"I hate that she found that envelope I got from Jules Bratman and destroyed it."

"It doesn't matter. I'll get some interns working on

pulling Ebony's case file from PACER. We'll have plenty of documentation when the story runs. Meanwhile, I'll get a camera crew on its way to record your account of things. I'll make sure that they bring hair and makeup with them, too, but resist the urge to get too glammed up. You've been through hell tonight. Make sure it shows, at least a little bit. It's better for the ratings, you know."

"Marisol," Rene said.

"Yeah, Rene?"

"Thanks for being such a crazy bitch. You saved my life. I owe you one."

Marisol went to her apartment and changed into some jeans and a T-shirt and grabbed her gun, a small, high-definition video camera, and a covert listening device before heading to Ebony Knight's home. She hadn't lied to Rene; she had every intention of calling the police to report what Carmelita had done. But before she did, she wanted to make sure she got every bit of dirt there was to get on Carmelita Sanchez.

"*I'm* the Queen of Miami News," Marisol said as she neared Ebony's home. "I'll be damned if I let Rene one-up me."

Marisol was nervous. The story Rene had told her about Carmelita's coldcocking her and holding her at gunpoint made her blood run cold. But if an assistant could tangle with Carmelita, so could she.

CHAPTER SIXTEEN

When Carmelita returned to Ebony's home, she stopped short in the foyer. Something seemed off. She couldn't put her finger on it, but something was different.

"Hello," she called out into the darkness.

Don't lose it, Carm, she told herself. *You're almost home free. Go upstairs, finish packing, and get the fuck out of Dodge before it's too late.*

Carmelita flicked the light switch. Nothing happened. She walked over to a lamp on an end table. Still nothing. A tiny inner voice told her to run, to turn around and leave while the getting was good, but she didn't listen to it. Instead she walked into the kitchen to flip the circuit breaker. As she reached out to the metal box that housed the breakers, she felt a sudden, searing pain radiate from her shoulder. Her vision went blurry, then her body dropped to the ground.

"Sleeper hold, bitch. Every good dominatrix should know it. You never know who might decide to buck the system." Ebony had been hiding in darkness, ready to take Carmelita down, and now she stood over Carmelita, who lay with her eyes closed, not moving.

Ebony looked in the cabinet under the sink. She extracted a roll of duct tape and went to work on Carmelita, putting a strip of the sticky, silver tape over her mouth before going around her wrists and ankles several times. Then she sat Carmelita's body in an upright position.

Ebony slapped Carmelita in the face to wake her. Carmelita opened her eyes and stared at her in mute confusion.

"Honey, I'm home. And you got some 'splaining to do," Ebony said with a Ricky Ricardo accent. "What's the matter, Carm? Didn't expect to see me? Thought you'd make a quick getaway?" Ebony asked with a smirk. "I don't think so!"

Ebony clocked Carmelita in the eye, yelling in rage as she did. She watched as the skin around Carmelita's eye began to quickly redden and swell up. Ebony could tell from the fiery look in Carmelita's good eye that she wanted to fight back, but she was immobile and wiggled around in frustration. Ebony threw her head back and laughed.

"Ooh, that's gonna leave a nasty bruise," Ebony said smugly. "But not to worry. You aren't going to have to worry about what you look like, and I'm pretty sure the mortician will be able to cover it up, if there's anything left of you when I'm done.

"Come on, on your feet." Ebony forced Carmelita to stand. Ebony made her hop from the kitchen into the living room and over to the couch, where she pushed her down onto it.

"Oh, Carmelita. You and I are going to have some fun. You're going to find out for yourself just how good of a dominatrix I was. See, I was an expert at inflicting pain. I'm going to take your mind and your body on the journey of a lifetime. I'm going to make you feel every bit of pain that I felt. But first, I've got some questions to ask that only you know the answers to."

Ebony spied a pack of cigarettes on the coffee table. She walked over and picked them up as Carmelita followed Ebony with her eyes.

"Still smoking, huh? I tried to quit myself but it was impossible, you know, with me being locked in Everglades and all. I had to do *something*."

Ebony tapped the pack on the back of her hand and extracted a cigarette. She lit it and inhaled deeply.

"I always did enjoy a good smoke. And who knew how much other people would enjoy watching me have a good smoke? I made so much money with the *Smoking Stocking* series. Before I went away, I'd sold over ten thousand copies of those DVDs. Yep . . . who knew how much money there was to be made?" Ebony sat down next to Carmelita on the couch.

"Oh, I think someone knew how much money I'd make. Yeah, Carmelita knew, didn't you, Carm?" Ebony flicked her ashes in Carmelita's face. She shook her head but the ashes tumbled from her forehead and the bridge of her nose into her eyes. Carmelita blinked violently as her eyes turned bloodshot.

"Stings, doesn't it?" Ebony chucked. "It's always so

hard to keep ashes out of your eyes when someone keeps flicking them in." Ebony punctuated her sentence with another flick of her cigarette.

"You know, you're such a fucking bitch. If you wanted to get paid, you just should have been a woman about yours and put in the work. Instead you had to use me, you lazy ho. Words can't even begin to describe how much I hate your ass!" Ebony shouted. Her hands were shaking and she wanted to wrap them around Carmelita's neck and squeeze the life out of her, but she resisted.

"Now I'm going to take this tape off your mouth while I ask you a few questions. Your ass better not scream. If you do, you're going to be very sorry. I'm packing heat, so don't get any crazy ideas. Make so much as a peep and you're going to get this square in your eye before I blast your ass. And trust me, if you don't like the way ashes feel, I can guarantee you that you're going to hate the way a lit cigarette followed by a bullet feels. Is that understood?"

Carmelita nodded. Ebony removed the duct tape from Carmelita's mouth.

"What do you want?" Carmelita asked immediately.

"What do I want?" Ebony was so angry she punched Carmelita again. "What the fuck do you think that I want? I want you dead!"

"You can't kill me."

"The hell I can't."

"There's the matter of thirteen million dollars. I have it and you want it. Plus there's all the money you had before you were committed, over one million dollars. I'm your conservator, the heir to your estate, remember? I control it all. If you want your money, I'm the only one who's going to be able to give it to you."

"That money was in a Swiss account," Ebony said, smiling.

Carmelita cut her off. "And it still is, just not in *your* Swiss account. Do you think that I couldn't find and access your money? Come on. I've found deeper hidden assets than yours. You're not nearly as clever as you think you are. So go ahead and kill me. But if you do, you will kill everything you ever worked for." Carmelita flashed Ebony a self-satisfied smile.

"No, Carmelita, you're the one who isn't as clever as she thinks. You see, I've already gotten my money."

"I don't believe you."

"Oh, believe it. You overestimate yourself. You're cocky. Just like you, I know all kinds of people that can help me out when I'm in a bind. It didn't even take a half hour for my little hacker friend to take care of the issue of putting *my* money where it rightfully belongs. And now we only have one issue left between us. You killed my mother, you killed my man, and you framed me. So I'm gonna make you suffer before I smoke your ass!"

Ebony took the lit end of her cigarette and placed it a millimeter away from Carmelita's cheek. "Such a pretty face. It's a shame what I'm going to have to do to it. Better not move not one bit. You're mighty close to this flame."

Carmelita didn't budge. Ebony grinned before pushing the cigarette into Carmelita's cheek, searing the skin. Carmelita let out a cry of anguish. Ebony punched Carmelita in the mouth, then spit in her face.

"I told you not to make a fucking peep."

"I should have let them lock your ass up. Your ass would be on death row," Carmelita mumbled.

"Coulda, shoulda, woulda, Carm. The fact remains that you didn't let them lock me up. And now look at you. Your face is burned, your eye is jacked up, and your lips look like Jay-Z's."

"You're right, Ebony. I didn't let them lock you up. What can I say? I guess I have a soft spot for you," Carmelita said sarcastically.

"Well, I don't have a soft spot for you. I hate you! And it's going to feel real good killing you."

"You don't have the balls," Carmelita challenged.

"You don't know the half of what I'm capable of," Ebony said before pounding Carmelita with her fists until she was unconscious.

Ebony went into the kitchen and filled a pitcher with freezing-cold water and ice, then grabbed a knife and a box of salt from the kitchen cabinet and went back into the living room. She doused Carmelita with the frigid water. Carmelita flinched but didn't open her eyes.

"Come on," Ebony said, slapping both Carmelita's cheeks and giving her shoulders a shake.

Carmelita squinted and blinked, her eyes fluttering open, then widening in horror. "Ebony?" She shook her head and water splashed everywhere. "What happened?"

"You got knocked the fuck out!" Ebony said with a cruel laugh, imitating Smokey from the movie *Friday*. "That's what happened."

"What are you doing here?"

"I'll give you a few seconds to let you get your wits about yourself," Ebony said mockingly. "It'll come back shortly."

"What do you want from me?" Carmelita asked innocently.

"What do I want from you? Okay, I'm tired of this. Cut the fake-amnesia bullshit, bitch, you know good and goddamned well what the fuck I want from you. I already told you so there's no sense in you trying to play the nut role. I want to know *why*," Ebony growled at Carmelita.

"Why what?" Carmelita asked, still the wide-eyed innocent, which enraged Ebony.

"Why are you acting like you don't know what the fuck I'm talking about, Carmelita? That shit isn't going to help you. I want to know why you fucked me over. What did I ever do to you to deserve what you did to me? Jeff, my mom, Erik, they didn't deserve to die. How could you do that to them? To me? And then you have the nerve to sit there and act all innocent and precious like you haven't done a goddamned thing."

A slow smirk spread across Carmelita's face. "You're a coward, Ebony. If you really wanted to avenge their deaths, you could have offed me in two seconds, but all you can do is sit here and whine like a little girl."

"That's where you're wrong. I'm going to kill you. But there are things I need to know. Tell me why, Carmelita!" Ebony demanded.

"Fuck it, you want to know why? I'll tell you why. Because I *could*. I saw an opportunity to make some money, and I wasn't going to let anyone or anything stand in my way," Carmelita spat, her dark eyes flashing deviously.

"But we'd made plenty money. You had three million from the blackmail hustle."

"It wasn't enough," Carmelita stated matter-of-factly.

"It never is with you, is it?"

"I guess not."

"I remember when your mother died and you got all that insurance money. You didn't share a dime with your sisters. You capitalized off your mother's murder. You should have helped her. Instead you just waited for her to be killed so you could come up. I should have known then that you were scandalous. Your own sister told me you were."

"Yeah, you *should* have known. It was nothing to let my family go. They actually thought they were going to hurt me by disowning me. But they got exactly what they deserved, which was nothing. They all sat around whispering and praying while Mama was getting her ass beat. I was the only one that told her to leave. I was the only one willing to make whatever sacrifices were needed so we could have a life without violence. But people had the nerve to act like I was crazy for telling her she shouldn't let some man love her with his fists.

She was weak and my sisters were weak, so if it's scandalous to say fuck 'em and forget 'em, then so be it."

"Carmelita, that's bullshit and we both know it. You didn't care about your mother, you just wanted her to do what you wanted. You're a coldhearted control freak."

"The way I see it is, you're with me or you're against me. They weren't with me. And being against me is the worst possible situation someone could put themselves in. I destroy my enemies completely and without mercy. But don't get self-righteous on me, Ebony. It's never enough for you either. I didn't have the market tapped on greed, now did I? You could have gotten the money for grad school and gotten out of the dominatrix business altogether, but you didn't do that, did you? You forgot all about wanting to become a psychiatrist once the money came pouring in."

Ebony sighed. Carmelita had a point, but none of that mattered.

"You know, if you hadn't gone and gotten engaged to Jeff, you would have never gotten into the mess your life became," Carmelita added.

"Don't you dare blame him for this! Don't you even speak his name!" Ebony yelled furiously. Ebony straddled Carmelita, her face barely an inch away from that of her nemesis. "You didn't know shit about him," Ebony growled.

"He had a penis. That's all I needed to know. They're all the same, Ebony, fuck what you say. He would have used you or cheated or hurt you—"

"Like you did?" Ebony asked, cutting Carmelita off.

Carmelita chuckled. "Ebony, you just don't get it, do you? There's no such thing as a good man. You saw it for yourself. I took Erik out when he could have killed Jeff or seriously hurt him or pressed charges or trashed his life. I helped your man out. Erik wanted to kill him. And how did your golden boy, Jeff, repay me? He was going to snitch on me. And no matter what anyone said, you were gonna get dragged down with me. Erik was your client, you were his beneficiary, and you were the one who blackmailed him. You were gonna go down in flames just like me, and it was going to be at the hands of your own man."

"Shut up!" Ebony screamed. She was pissed as hell because Carmelita was probably right. Jeff wasn't going to let Carmelita get away with murdering someone right in front of him, and she would have gone down with Carmelita.

"I was protecting you, Ebony, but you were too stupid to see it. If I hadn't been there, who knows what Erik would have done to you. I loved you, girl. I loved you more than my own flesh-and-blood sisters. You were my *familia*. You say I turned on you; well, I say that you turned on me!"

"What we were doing, it wasn't right," Ebony said, shaking her head as if that could block Carmelita's words from entering it. Carmelita was twisting and distorting things.

"Who's to be the judge of whether what we were

doing was right or wrong? Haven't you ever heard the phrase 'Only God can judge me'?" Carmelita asked with a smirk.

"Carmelita, Tupac is the last person you need to be quoting right now."

"Ebony, if I hadn't done what I did, we'd have both gotten the death penalty. This is Florida. Two black women, one of whom happens to be the daughter of a con artist, the other one Dominican . . . are you kidding? They'd have put us *under* the jail. They'd have executed us, revived us, and executed us again for fucking over a man like Erik Johansen. Fuck what you've heard, this is still a white man's world."

"Is that the best that you can do, play the race card? I expected more from a conniving, scheming bitch like you."

"Ebony, look, I know what I did was wrong. I know that you're going to kill me, and I probably deserve everything that you're going to do to me and then some. But I just want you to know that I still love you, you're still my sister, and I'm so sorry. I never wanted you to get hurt. That's why I protected you. I could have let you get sent up the river. Instead I got you put in Everglades. It was only going to be until you came to your senses. At the end of the ninety days things would have been different."

"Carmelita, spare me the bullshit. You didn't have to drag my mother into any of this. You didn't have to kill her," Ebony said, feeling her blood boil. She slapped

Carmelita hard across the face with the back of her hand.

Carmelita didn't flinch, she just glared at Ebony coldly before saying, "Fuck your mother."

"What was that? What did you say?" Ebony asked, bending her ear down in front of Carmelita. "I know you didn't just say fuck my mother." Swiftly she took the knife and slit a gash on the side of Carmelita's face, through the spot where she'd burned her earlier. Carmelita's agony-filled screams reverberated off the walls.

"Fuck my mother?" Ebony asked with a laugh. "Really? No, fuck you!" Ebony poured salt directly onto Carmelita's wound, then used her palm to grind the stinging granules in.

"That's how my heart feels, Carmelita. That's exactly how my heart feels on a good day. But, oh, you haven't begun to feel the pain of my bad days. But you will, Carmelita. We're just getting started."

A half hour Ebony had sliced Carmelita's skin in a dozen places, rubbing salt in all her wounds. Ebony turned up the stereo to drown out Carmelita's screams as she watched her nemesis reduced to a crying, bloody wreck.

"You don't have the guts to kill me," Carmelita whispered, her voice hoarse.

"And you don't have the strength to kill me," Ebony scoffed. "Look at you. You're a hot mess. And I can't believe the cojones on you, bitch. You're still talking shit after all this."

"You're pussyfooting around with this torture bullshit. I said it before and I'll say it again, you're a coward. You got me with my hands taped behind my back. If you were a woman about yours, we'd have gone toe-to-toe."

"Carmelita, you're one to talk. Your whole life you used people. You used Amber, you used me, you even used your mother's death. Instead of helping your mother get out of an abusive relationship, you let her get killed, all so you could get the insurance money. And you want to talk about somebody being a coward. Ha! What have you ever really done that took any bravery?"

"Fuck bravery! I helped make you rich. And you want to talk about brave, I killed Erik for you. He was going to do who knows what to you and that sorry-ass man of yours, and I saved you. I took care of things. I looked out for you."

"And then when I wouldn't do what you wanted, you flipped. And you killed my man and my mother. There's no excuse, Carmelita, there's just no excuse. But you know what? I'm getting just as tired of this as you are. I know you're hoping for a quick and painless death, but it ain't gonna happen. I could shoot you in the head, but I'm not going to. You know stabbing is extra fucking personal. So it's time for it all to come to an end. Say good night, Carm." Ebony grabbed the knife she'd tortured Carmelita with and held it high in the air, watching the look of sheer terror in Carmelita's eyes as she prepared to stab Carmelita in her cold, black heart.

Then the doorbell rang.

CHAPTER SEVENTEEN

I f you think that you're saved by the bell, you're dead-ass wrong," Ebony said to Carmelita, replacing her duct tape. "We're going to wait for whoever is there to go away. And then you die."

The doorbell rang two more times. Then the knocking began, first on the door and then on the windows.

Maybe Monk came back, Ebony thought. She was about to peek out the blinds when she heard someone calling her name. It wasn't Monk.

"Ebony! Ebony!" a voice called loudly from outside the open window. "E-12!" the voice yelled. "E-12, it's me, K-17!"

Ebony's eyes widened. It couldn't be! She peeked out of the window near the front door. No one was there. She ran through the kitchen and peered out the blinds looking onto the patio.

"Kira!" Ebony gasped, flinging open the back door. "What the hell are you doing here?"

"Are you going to leave me standing outside or are you going to let me in?"

Ebony gaped at the waiflike woman standing in front of her. She was bloody. Her long hair was all over her head, and she had a wild look in her eyes that Ebony had seen many times before. She grabbed Kira by the wrist and pulled her inside, praying that no one had seen her.

"I don't understand." Ebony was flabbergasted.

"What's to understand, E-12?" Kira asked, shrugging her thin shoulders.

"How did you know where I lived?"

"Please, I know everything about my sisters from Funkanova. Remember my husband, Jenkins, from Everglades? May he rest in peace," Kira said, crossing herself. "Well, he told me a lot about you. I hope you aren't mad. I'm so happy to see you!" Kira chattered, giving Ebony a big bear hug.

"Slow down, Kira," Ebony said, holding her at arm's length.

"K-17, remember?" Kira had insisted on being called K-17 and on calling Ebony E-12 when they bunked together at the psychiatric hospital.

Ebony rolled her eyes. "K-17, I thought you were dead. You ran back into the burning building."

"I didn't do that. I know you thought I was dead, but as you can see, I'm not. I told you, the old fakerooni works every time. Every single time. I ran back to look at my handiwork. That was the best fire I'd ever set. Come on, do you really think I'd go on some suicide mission after *finally* getting out? Only a crazy person would do that, and remember, we're not crazy."

Ebony cut Kira off before she could go off on a tangent, which she was prone to do. "How did you know I'd be here?"

"I didn't but I took a chance. It made sense you'd come home. Anyway, I went on my bloodthirst. But I guess you can see that. I didn't really feel like cleaning up. Well, actually that's not entirely accurate. See, after I killed my parents, I had to keep their blood on my hands. It's a symbolic gesture."

"You killed your parents?"

"Naturally. They were the source of all my problems. You have to pull a weed out by the root or else it'll grow back even worse. But my parents weren't the only weeds in my garden. Oh, no! I also killed my old doctor plus a few people that got in my way, like this trucker that picked me up. Ooh, and I set a car on fire near the federal building because, see, it's the government's fault that I was locked up. I showed them! I got them all back!"

Ebony paced back and forth. "What is it that you want from me?"

"I want you to come back to the nebula with me, silly."

There was a crash in the living room.

"What was that?" Kira asked, trying to look around Ebony and into the living room. "Is that the bitch you wanted revenge against?"

"Yes, Kira. I was just getting ready to take care of her when you came."

"Cool. Now we can kill her together!" Kira barked like an excited puppy.

"No, Kira. I've got to do this on my own. Why don't you do me a favor and sit down at the kitchen table. I'll be right back."

Kira looked disappointed but did what Ebony asked of her. When Ebony returned to the living room, she found Carmelita on the floor, attempting to crawl over to the phone.

"Oh, no, you don't!" Ebony said, kicking Carmelita in the ribs. She cut the duct tape from around Carmelita's ankles and pulled her to her feet. "Come on, Carmelita. Up the stairs you go."

Carmelita didn't move.

Ebony poked her in the back with the knife. "I said move! And don't even think of making a run for it, because this knife isn't the only weapon I have. I've got a gun on me and I won't hesitate to use it."

Carmelita trudged up the stairs and into Ebony's bedroom. Ebony pushed the half-packed suitcase off the bed, then pushed Carmelita onto it. Then she sat on her chest. Carmelita squirmed and kicked.

"Stop moving. I know it's scary as hell to look death in the face. You want to fight. But give it up. It's over. That wasn't the police or anyone else coming to rescue you. That was my old roommate from the mental hospital, Kira. We escaped together and she's as crazy as they come. As a matter of fact, she wanted to rush right in and kill you herself. But I'm going to do that."

Ebony removed the tape from Carmelita's mouth. "Do you have anything to say for yourself before I kill you?"

"Ebony, you might kill me, but you're never going to get away with it. The police are going to lock you up.

You may even get the death penalty. So I won't be walking into death alone. I'll be holding your hand."

Ebony laughed. "I may as well be dead already. After all, you took my life, remember? But the funny thing is I finally realized something about you. You're afraid. For all the bravado and swagger you seemed to have mastered, I see now that all along you've been afraid."

"Of what?"

"Of life. That's why your solution to everything is death. You're so afraid of losing, of there being something that you can't win, that you'll kill before you allow yourself to fail."

"Don't try your armchair psychiatry on me!" Carmelita hissed.

"Nope, I'm right on point. Right now you're afraid of death. I can see it in your eyes. I can hear it in your voice. You're just this close away from begging for your life, and I'm loving every single second of it."

"Ebony, listen to me. Things have gone too far, but it isn't too late. It isn't too late for the both of us to walk away from this. We'll go our separate ways and pretend we never met. You want the money? Fine! I'll give you the money."

Ebony threw her head back and roared with laughter. "Bitch, please! I *already* have my money, remember? Looks like you have nothing left to barter with."

"You don't really want to do this. I can tell."

"You know what, Carm? You're right. I *don't* really want to do this. I've already got so much blood on my

hands. I already know how it feels to take away someone's life, and unlike you, I hate the feeling. But that's
the cross that I'm going to have to bear. Me."

"Ebony, please. You want me to beg? I'll beg. Please,
don't kill me. Please, let me live. I'll even help you get off
for real this time."

Ebony looked into Carmelita's pleading brown eyes,
holding her face in her hands. She kissed her bloody
cheek and brought the knife to Carmelita's neck.

"There was a time when I loved you like a sister. I had
your back and I thought that you had mine. But then you
threw it all away. And now, it's over. Good-bye, Carm."

Ebony nearly gagged as she grabbed Carmelita by the
hair and dragged the knife across her neck. Ebony felt the
skin and muscle tearing beneath the blade as she cut into
the cartilage of Carmelita's windpipe. There was a sound
that reminded Ebony of a balloon being deflated. The
sound was followed by gasping and gurgling. Carmelita's
eyes bulged as blood poured from her gaping wound
onto Ebony's four-hundred-thread-count Pratesi sheets.

Ebony dropped the knife on the bed. She tried frantically to wipe the blood from her hands, but it seemed
that the harder she tried, the more the blood seemed to
smear and spread. She stepped back and looked at the
mess she'd made. Carmelita was finally dead.

Ebony asked herself if it was all worth it. She would
have to answer the question after she'd gone as far as $14
million could take her.

★ ★ ★

Kira was filled with nervous energy, something that always happened when she went off her meds; to call her manic would be an understatement.

"Ebony needs to hurry up and kill her enemy so we can continue with the plan. This is going to be so hot! I'm going back to the nebula and I'm going to take my sister E-12 with me. She doesn't know that the only way to access the portal back to the motherland is through her death, but that's just a technicality. I'm sure she'll be down with the program."

Kira decided to go upstairs and check on her friend. After all, there was no telling what could be going on up there; Ebony might need her help.

"Ebony!" Kira yelled as she found her way upstairs to Ebony's locked bedroom door. "Are you okay in there?"

Moments later Ebony peeked out of her bedroom door, a towel wrapped around her body. "What's going on? I thought I told you to chill."

"I am," Kira explained. "But I think we better hurry up and get out of here."

"Kira, you don't have to stay here. You're free to leave whenever you want."

"No, I can't. I want you to come back to the nebula with me. You'll be safe there."

"Kira, I think that it's best we go our separate ways," Ebony said gently. "Nothing personal or anything, but I move better on my own."

"But there's strength in numbers, E-12. We should band together," Kira insisted.

"Kira, let me take a quick shower and get dressed, and then we'll figure it out. In the meantime, you should go downstairs."

Kira smiled. "Does that mean you're going to come with me?"

"Sure, Kira."

"Cool!"

Kira went back downstairs and walked around the lower level of Ebony's house, peeking out the closed blinds and curtains. She could have sworn that she detected motion outside one of the windows. Kira went into the kitchen and got a knife, then slipped out the back door to investigate, tiptoeing around the house. She went a few steps, then stopped short. In the darkness Kira could make out a woman hiding in the shrubs.

"Who the hell are you?" Kira shrieked upon discovering Marisol Rivera-Frye crouched behind a shrub.

"I, I'm from the gas company," Marisol lied, stammering nervously. "There's been a report of a natural-gas leak in the neighborhood, so I'm investigating."

"At two o'clock in the morning? I don't think so. Nuh-uh! And you don't look like any gas-company employee that I've ever seen."

"I am with the gas company, and I'm all done here, so I'll just be on my way." Marisol turned to walk away.

Kira grabbed her by the arm. "If you're with the gas company, then where's your truck?"

"I parked it down the street. I've been on foot going door-to-door."

"Bullshit!" Kira yelled, holding up the knife. "You're going to come inside this house and start talking about what you're doing here, Marisol Rivera-Frye. Oh, yeah, I know exactly who you are. If you don't, I'll shove this knife right into your heart."

"Okay, okay," Marisol said quickly. "I'm going."

"E-12! Come downstairs! There's been a breach in security!" Kira yelled.

"Kira, what the hell is going on?" Ebony asked, walking into the kitchen dressed in a pair of jeans and a T-shirt.

"That's what I've been trying to figure out!" Kira said. "I found that bitch Marisol Rivera-Frye from the news outside with a video camera snooping on us. She tried to tell me some lame story about being with the gas company, but I know that's a lie. So spill it. Tell us why you're here or I'm going to slit your throat."

"Kira, are you crazy? Put the knife down," Ebony commanded. Kira didn't budge. "K-17, put the knife down now."

Kira looked disappointed but put the knife down on the table. Ebony grabbed it and tossed it into the sink.

"I can't believe this," Marisol whispered in shock. "Ebony Knight alive and in the flesh. Rene was right on the money."

"Who's Rene?" Kira asked. "Is she a *chupacabra* killer? Because I'm telling you now I'm immortal. You can't kill me. We don't die, we multiply!"

"Kira, will you chill the fuck out?" Ebony asked. "Marisol, what the hell are you doing here?"

"I want to ask you the same thing," Marisol replied. "But I think my assistant already figured it out. You're here to get revenge on Carmelita Sanchez. She set you up and had you sent to Everglades, and now it's payback time."

"You damn right it's payback time," Kira said. "Ebony, did you kill that bitch already?"

"Kira, I want you to go into the living room," Ebony said, not taking her eyes off Marisol. "I want to talk to Marisol alone."

"Oh, I get it," Kira said. "You want to off her yourself. You're so selfish. I've only killed six people today and my bloodthirst still needs to be quenched. I don't understand why you won't let me help you. We both know that you're not a killer. I'm a killer! You really should let me get rid of this nosy bitch."

"K-17," Ebony said. "Go in the living room, sit down, and watch TV or something. This won't take very long."

"Fine," Kira sulked. "I'll let you kill this one. But if there's anyone else who needs handling before we go back to Funkanova, you're going to let me take care of it. Otherwise you and I are going to have some real problems."

Kira walked into the living room and Ebony pulled

out the gun Monk had given her from her waistband. Marisol gasped.

"Look, I don't want to hurt you, but I will if I have to. Don't make any sudden moves and you'll be okay. Now tell me what you're doing here." Ebony took a seat at the kitchen table across from Marisol and pointed the gun at her.

"The same thing you are. Trying to make sure that Carmelita Sanchez goes down."

"Why would you want to do that?"

"For one, I know that she's the true murderer of Erik Johansen, Jeff Cardoza, and your mother. Second, she tried to kill my assistant, Rene, tonight and make it look like a suicide."

"She did what?"

"Rene figured out everything. We know that you were never mentally ill and that the papers that got you committed were fake. The letter you sent from Everglades made it into the hands of an attorney by the name of Jules Bratman. My assistant saw it. She called the doctor at the hospital you were supposed to have been treated at in the past, and it turns out that he's been dead for years. He couldn't have possibly given anyone any information about you. When she came here to get more information, Carmelita tried to kill her. If I hadn't gone to check on her, she would have died."

"I'm sorry to hear all that, but now that you've figured all this out, do you think that I can let you leave this house alive? You know too much."

"Yes, Ebony, you can let me leave this house alive. Ebony, let me help you. I can tell your story; I can get the truth out there."

"You can't help me. Nobody can help me."

"I can and I will. Look, I'm not going to lie and say that helping you isn't going to help me, too. This is the story of the year, maybe even the decade. I want to be the one to break it. This is Emmy material."

"Forgive me for not giving a flying fuck about you winning a goddamned Emmy."

"Please," Marisol begged.

"Marisol, you seem like a smart woman. And you're an ambitious sister. I like that. But there are things that you don't know."

"What things? That Carmelita is probably in this house somewhere dead? Don't you think that I figured all of that out? I don't care about that. I know how crazy she is. I can't blame you for wanting to kill her, and as far as I'm concerned, that shit is between the two of you. I just want the story." Marisol looked Ebony squarely in the eyes.

"It sounds good, but for all I know you'll flip the script on me. I just can't take that chance."

"If you try to escape now, chances are you're going to get caught. If you let me tell your story, I'll back you up. I can tell the police anything that you want me to. I can say that Kira did it all. I'll say that she kidnapped you from the hospital, went on a killing spree, and she's responsible for Carmelita's death."

"Is that right?" Kira asked angrily, standing in the doorway. "You bitches in here plotting and scheming on me?"

"Kira, calm down," Ebony said.

"Fuck you, Ebony. I will not calm down. I came here to help you and you're in here plotting to cross me."

"I'm not plotting shit but getting out of here. I've done what I needed to do."

"I thought you said that you were going to the nebula with me," Kira said. "You lied to me!"

"We can't just let her go! She's crazy! She's a menace to society," Marisol balked.

"There's no *we*. It's every woman for herself," Ebony said.

"If you run, it's going to make you look even more suspicious than you already do. No one will believe you. The solution I offered is the only way," Marisol said.

"I'm tired of you!" Kira screamed, rushing at Marisol. Marisol's reflexes went into overdrive. She grabbed her chair and hurled it at Kira, knocking her to the floor. Ebony stared at the scene, unsure what to do.

"Ebony, you'd better choose and choose quickly. If you aren't on my side, you're on hers, and I'll make sure that the both of you go down in flames," Marisol threatened.

"Neither of you are going to stand in my way," Ebony said. "I don't want to kill you, but I will."

Kira got up quickly and leaped at Ebony.

"You dirty bitch! You promised me you'd go back to Funkanova with me!"

The two of them wrestled on the floor, struggling for possession of the gun. Marisol headed toward the door.

"She's getting away," Kira said angrily. *"Chupacabra!"* she yelled, taking a bite of Ebony's cheek. Ebony yelped and grabbed her bleeding face, and Kira grabbed the gun. She fired a shot in the air and Marisol stopped in her tracks.

"Both of you bitches sit the fuck down!" Kira yelled. "Now I'm going back to the nebula, and I'll kill anyone that stands in my way! They're not taking me back to some hospital. I said sit the fuck down!"

Ebony and Marisol sat down in the kitchen chairs.

"E-12, why did you do that?" Kira asked angrily. "How could you turn on me after everything I did to help you?"

"Kira, I didn't turn on you. You're just too sick to see the truth."

"I'm not sick! You're sick," Kira waved the gun around. "I didn't want to have to kill you, but you gave me no choice."

"Hey, Kira, is it? Look, I didn't mean those things you heard me say to Ebony a few minutes ago. I was just telling Ebony what she wanted to hear so that she wouldn't kill me. But I'm not like her. I want to go back to the nebula with you. It sounds like a lovely place," Marisol said.

"How do I know that you're not telling me what you think I want to hear now? You're a reporter. The media is full of wolves and liars."

"I'm not like them," Marisol said. "Why don't you put down the gun so we can go there."

"Oh, no! I'm not falling for that."

"Fine then. Don't put down the gun. Let's just go there."

"But you don't understand, Marisol. You have to leave your earthly body behind to get there. I'm going to have to kill you, I'm even going to have to kill myself in order to go back."

Marisol began to cry.

"Don't cry, Marisol," Kira said soothingly. "It's not going to hurt. It's going to be the best thing that ever happened to you. Now I want the both of you to get up and take all your clothes off."

"I'm not doing shit," Ebony said.

"Oh, yes, you are, Ebony. You'd better! If you don't want to suffer the punishment usually reserved for traitors, you'll do exactly what I say. This is your road to atonement. You'll thank me."

Ebony didn't move.

Kira walked over to her and pointed the gun in her face. "Do it!" Kira yelled.

"Please, Ebony," Marisol begged. "Just do what she says."

Marisol stood and began removing her clothing.

Ebony shook her head and followed suit. *As soon as I get a chance, I'm going to take this bitch.*

"Do you have any candles?" Kira asked.

"I don't know," Ebony said. "I haven't been living

here, remember? I've been locked down in Everglades with you."

"Then look for them. Where did you keep them before?"

"There were some decorative ones around the house. I kept tea lights and votives under the sink."

"Then get them."

Kira kept the gun pointed toward Ebony and Marisol while Ebony fetched the candles.

"Good. Now I want you to grab anything that can start a fire. Lighter fluid, aerosol cans, and whatever else you can find," Kira said to Marisol. Marisol moved around the kitchen, crying and naked but doing what she was told.

"Now let's go upstairs and take care of Carmelita," Kira said.

"She's already dead," Ebony reminded her.

"I didn't say we were going to kill her. I said we were going to take care of her. We've got to banish her soul to Hades before we can go to Funkanova."

Kira forced Ebony and Marisol to go upstairs and into the bedroom. Marisol screamed when she saw Carmelita's corpse.

"Don't be a baby," Kira said. "Now pour the liquids all over her."

Marisol sniffled as she did what she was told. Kira sang a song in gibberish while she did, dancing and taking her clothes off.

" 'Our Father, who art in heaven,' " Marisol prayed softly.

"Stop that!" Kira yelled at her. "We don't pray to fathers! We're goddesses!"

Marisol stopped praying.

"Kira, enough already," Ebony said. "Let her go. She doesn't have anything to do with this. I'm the one you really want to go back with you."

"That's true. But this is even better, can't you see? There are three of us now. Three is the magic number. Yes, it is."

Ebony rolled her eyes and Marisol began to cry again. Kira pulled a box of matches out of her pocket and set Ebony's bed on fire.

"Now come on downstairs."

"But the fire," Marisol began.

"Don't worry about the fire. It's a source of purification. We need it. Besides, who cares if this house burns down? It was desecrated. Now it'll be sanctified."

Pointing the gun at Ebony and Marisol, Kira made them go back downstairs.

Marley pulled up in front of Ebony's home. She'd contemplated staking out the house as she and Rocky had done earlier, but was tired of playing a passive role. She wanted to prove once and for all that she was right about Carmelita Sanchez, and she couldn't do that sitting in her car. She walked to the house and thought she smelled smoke, but figured that she'd been on the scene of so many fires that day that the scent was still lingering in her nose.

She tried peeking in the front window, but the drapes were closed. She stood on her tiptoes and attempted to peek inside the glass panel on the front window. She was too short. Marley tried the knob. The door was locked. She walked around to the back of the house and tried the back door. It was unlocked. Marley knew that entering a private home without a search warrant was against the law and that she could lose her job, but she felt it was necessary. If her theory was correct and Ebony Knight was inside, she'd be stopping a homicide. The way Marley saw things, that constituted probable cause.

Marley pulled out her gun and slipped into the house silently. This time she knew that her mind wasn't playing tricks on her. She could definitely smell smoke and the smoke detector was blaring. Marley slunk with her back against the wall toward the interior of the house to get a better look at things.

"What the fuck?" Marley whispered. Dozens of candles were burning everywhere, and she saw three naked women in the middle of the living room. One of them was Kira Long, dancing around and saying something incoherent while holding a gun. The second one appeared to be Marisol Rivera-Frye, the reporter, and she was crying uncontrollably. The third woman was Ebony Knight, who had a look on her face that could cut glass. Clouds of black smoke were billowing from upstairs.

"Please, Kira, just let us go," Marisol begged. "We're going to be burned alive."

Marley aimed her gun at Kira. She didn't have a clear shot because Kira kept moving around erratically.

Shit! Marley thought. She pulled out her cell phone and whispered into it. Then she walked slowly into the living room.

"Miami Beach Police!" Marley shouted. "Kira, put the gun down and your hands where I can see them."

The smoke was getting thicker and Marley had a difficult time seeing.

"No one is taking me back!" Kira yelled.

In that instant Marley knew that Kira was going to start shooting. Kira spun around, firing randomly. Marley crouched low and fired back, hitting Kira in the leg. Marley fired again, this time hitting Kira in the chest. She fell to the floor.

"Is everyone okay?" Marley asked, coughing and covering her face and mouth with her shirt. There was no answer. Marley walked over to Kira's body and kicked the gun out of her reach.

"I'm getting out of here!" Marisol screamed hysterically. She'd reached the front door and was about to run out. Ebony didn't answer.

"Ebony," Marley said, rushing to her side. Ebony didn't move. "Ebony." Still no answer. Marley bent down next to Ebony and noticed the pool of blood forming beneath her. She was hit.

"I need a bus!" Marley shouted into her cell phone, giving Ebony Knight's address.

"Marisol! I need some help here," Marley called out, but there was no answer. Marisol had already run out of the house stark naked and screaming.

Marley knew that she shouldn't move an injured person, but she had to act quickly. She'd called for backup and a fire truck, but the smoke was getting thicker, and in the midst of the melee, several candles had been knocked over, setting the lower level of the house on fire. She put her gun back in her holster and grabbed Ebony beneath her underarms, dragging her around the burning furniture and out the front door.

Once Ebony was a safe distance from the house, Marley ran to her car and grabbed her gym bag and an emergency first-aid kit from the trunk. She pulled a blanket out of the first-aid kit and covered Ebony's naked body. She checked Ebony's pulse and breathing. She was alive, but barely.

"Hold on, Ebony. You're going to make it. Just hold on."

Marley caught up to Marisol, who was still hysterical, grabbing her by the shoulders.

"Marisol, I need you to calm down. Here, put these clothes on!" Marley ordered, unzipping her gym bag and handing Marisol some workout clothes. Marisol stared at Marley blankly. "Marisol, do it now. The neighbors are looking."

A small crowd had begun to gather outside their homes, pointing at the scene. Marisol looked around at the people staring at her and did as she was told. The paramedics arrived shortly thereafter and hoisted Ebony onto a gurney, hooking her up to an IV and putting an oxygen mask over her face.

"Is she going to be okay?" Marley asked the medic.

"Too soon to tell."

"Keep me posted," Marley said, giving the medic her card and watching the ambulance take Ebony away.

Marley walked over to Marisol, who was being tended to by a second paramedic unit. "Are you all right?"

"About as well as I can be considering what I've been through," Marisol said.

"I'm going to need you to tell me exactly what happened," Marley said.

"It's such a long story."

"I've got time."

Marisol explained Rene's confrontation with Carmelita to Marley.

"So instead of calling the authorities, you decided to confront Carmelita Sanchez yourself, even though you knew she'd committed several felonies? Do you realize how stupid that was?"

"I do. I was going to call the cops, I just wanted to make sure I got the exclusive before I did. I apologize for the trouble I caused and I thank you for saving my life."

Marley nodded.

"How did you know what was going on? Did Rene call you?" Marisol asked.

"No. Let's just say I had a hunch and I had to follow it." Marley understood how Marisol and Rene could be so compelled by Ebony's story that they'd risk anything to learn the truth. "What exactly were you all doing in there naked?"

"Kira made us do that. She insisted that she was going back to some place called Funkanova and was taking us with her. She made Ebony and I get naked and then set Carmelita Sanchez on fire."

"Do you know who killed Carmelita?"

"I don't. She was already dead when I got there." Marisol started to cry. "I didn't even know that she was there until Kira went berserk."

"If I have any more questions, I'll talk to you later." Grilling Marisol wasn't going to make any difference. Marley would never get the satisfaction of seeing Carmelita Sanchez prosecuted, but she'd done some good nonetheless. She saved the lives of two people and stopped a fugitive on a killing spree. And whether she could prove it or not, she knew that she'd solved the case of the Ebony Knight murders.

EPILOGUE

When I woke *up in the hospital, I thought for a moment that everything that had transpired had been some kind of dream and that I was still in Everglades. Something was restraining my right arm, and I thought I was still handcuffed to my bed. But that wasn't the case. Monk was sitting there beside me, holding my hand.*

"What happened?" we asked each other at the same time.

"You first," I said. "How are Miss Cat and Nu-Nu? Did you save them?"

"They're gone."

I don't know why but my eyes immediately filled with tears. "Gone?"

"They were already dead when I got the phone call. It was a setup. My mother, my brother, my aunt, they were all killed, but I don't want to talk about that now."

I nodded. I knew exactly what he was going through.

"You feel okay?" he asked.

"I guess, I'm a little groggy."

"You must have a lucky horseshoe up your ass. The bullet

went in and out. A quarter of an inch to the right and the bullet would have hit your spinal cord."

"How do you know all this?"

"I paid a nurse to get me the information and to let me come in here with you."

"Why?"

"I don't know, Ebony. I saw the story on the news and I just wanted to make sure that you were okay. Marisol Rivera-Frye and some chick named Rene Fields gave one helluva report."

"Is that the only reason you're here holding my hand?" I asked, smiling at Monk.

"Nah, that's not the only reason. You know why I'm here."

"Yeah, I know," I said, squeezing his hand.

"The truth is, I don't know where else to go. I don't have anyone left."

"That's not true. You've got me. That is, if you want me."

"I don't know what I want right now," Monk said.

"That's okay. Neither do I. But maybe we can keep each other company while we figure it out."

"Ebony, how are you feeling?" Marley Parnell was standing next to my bed.

"So we meet again," I said.

"We do indeed."

"Where's your partner? You here to play good cop, bad cop? Let me guess, am I getting ready to go to jail for something?"

"My partner won't be coming inside. I wanted to talk to you alone."

"What am I being charged with this time?"

"You're not charged with anything."

"For now."

"More than likely for good," Marley said. "Unless you have something you want to confess to."

"I don't have anything to tell you but the truth. Kira Long set Everglades on fire. I didn't touch a single match. But I did use her act of arson to escape. I told you the first time I met you that I didn't kill Erik Johansen and my Jeff. And I told you I didn't belong in a mental hospital chained to my bed like a dog. But you didn't believe me."

"Ebony, you don't know what I believed. The fact of the matter is that I always thought that there was more to the story than what you were telling. I just didn't know what. My partner and my captain, they're the ones who were out for blood. I just wanted to get to the truth."

"Well, do you think you know it?"

"Yeah. I think you went to Carmelita's—"

"I went home. That was my house," I said, correcting her.

"I'm sorry. You're right. That was your home. I don't know if you know, but it was destroyed in the fire."

I nodded.

"I think you went to confront her because she more than likely is the true killer of Erik Johansen, Jeff Cardoza, and your mother. A reporter, Rene Fields, got wind of a letter you sent while you were detained."

Marley explained to me the ordeal that Rene had gone through.

"Carmelita isn't more than likely the killer, she is the killer," I said.

"Then I have one question to ask you."

"Go ahead."

"Did you kill Carmelita Sanchez?"

"No. She and Amber were dead when I got there. Kira killed them."

"Why was Kira at your house?"

"She was crazy. I don't know why she did anything that she did."

"You know, Ebony, I don't believe you. I think you killed Carmelita Sanchez."

"So what are you going to do?"

"Nothing. It's over. You've already lost enough. Have a nice life," Marley said, but not with an attitude. She said it as if she meant it.

After I was *released from the hospital, Monk and I got on the first plane smoking to Brazil. We stayed in Rio for a while, but the fast pace wasn't exactly what we were looking for, so eventually we rented a cottage in Salvador da Bahia. But while we were in Rio, we visited the famous humongous statue of Jesus, Christ the Redeemer. We took the train up Corcovado Mountain shortly before sunset, and it seemed as if everyone left as soon as we got there. As dusk approached, we were practically alone, watching as the sun disappeared over the horizon,* *streaking the sky in shades of orange, red, and purple. It was one of the most beautiful and powerful sights I'd ever witnessed. Monk fell on his knees, and I knelt beside him.*

"Are you a Christian?" Monk asked me.

"I guess."

"There's no guess. You either are or you aren't."

"I know what being a Christian means, but I've just never been a religious woman. In fact, I spent a lot of my life being downright blasphemous. I called myself a goddess and expected the world to worship me, and I didn't mean it figuratively, I was as literal as it gets. I thought I was too large and too powerful to fall, but I learned the hard way that I'm human. There's got to be someone more powerful than me that's been showing me grace and mercy through all of this. I think it's Jesus."

"I thought I was a Christian. But I've done a lot that I'm ashamed of. I hope God forgives me."

"Are you ever going to talk about what happened?" I asked. Monk still hadn't gone into great detail surrounding Miss Cat and Nuquan's deaths, but every now and then he'd let a little something slip, usually when he was feeling particularly sad.

"Maybe," he said, staring up at the statue.

Monk closed his eyes and held my hand as I prayed with him. I asked for forgiveness for all the things we'd done in our lives. Between the two of us I was sure we had a list as long as the trek up the mountain. I begged God to wash the blood from our hands, to wipe the slate clean, and help us find a way to go on with our lives. We cried and prayed until a woman told us that the last train down the mountain was leaving.

I saw the lights twinkling in a favela in the distance and thought about the families, the mothers and children, who resided there. All they had was each other, and yet they found a way to be happy. If only our mothers could have found that kind of happiness in the simple things in life, they'd probably still be with us. Instead we relied on money and material things to define who we were and how we felt, and we paid a higher price for those worldly things than we could ever have imagined.

Being in Brazil, I can't help but be reminded me of a scene from the movie Black Orpheus, a movie that my mother and I used to watch together when I was a little girl. The hero of the story is told that he can have the love of his life, who died, back again as long as he doesn't look back. He does, and he loses his love forever. So I try not to think about the past. I try to appreciate that I have a friend like Monk with me on this journey forward. But there isn't a day that goes by that I don't think of my mother and Jeff and all the love that had once been a part of my life. There also isn't a day that goes by that I don't blame myself for their deaths. No matter how evil and self-serving Carmelita was, it was my darkness, my greed, that killed them. But after receiving Christ's redemption, I will hopefully find my way through the darkness and be able to move on without looking back.